Retro '84

ONE FAN'S LOVE LETTER TO NINTENDO®

By Mike Pensinger

Retro '84

One Fan's Love Letter to Nintendo®

Printed in United States of America

ISBN: 979-8-99-006780-6

Pensinger Press
Lemont, Illinois

First Edition: 2024

In 1983 the video game industry crashed. What if it stayed that way and never recovered? Ario has the most important job interview of his life (and our lives, too). The resurrection of an entire video game industry depends on it . . . but he must get there first. Come run, jump, hit, swing, slash, kick, smash, grab, and shoot to uncover, search, discover, find, and explore—in a first-of-its-kind book—one Nintendo® fan's love letter to an industry deeply impactful to him and to billions of others over nearly a half-century. Blow into the cartridge, pop it in, and power on. . . .

Can you find all of the Easter eggs?

Dedication

To a young boy who fell in love
with Zelda (the game, not Princess)

Prologue

Throughout the history of video games, a dark chapter exists that, like most crashes, came suddenly and on the heels of great success. Leaving behind a path of destruction was one thing, but the uncertainty of the industry's future was far more troubling. During the late 1970s and early 1980s, video games were experiencing a meteoric rise in popularity. Arcades bustled with the sounds and sights brought forth by great technical and design creativity while rabid gamers lined up to pump quarters into their favorite machines. But beneath the surface of a rapid ascent, a precipitous fall was coming, a cautionary tale of how the seemingly invincible gaming industry teetered on the brink of extinction.

Out of the 1970s and into the early 1980s, the video game marketplace featured several in-home video game consoles missing the mark as the follow-up to the earlier golden age of arcade games. Made possible by technological advancements in the form of greater computing power at lower costs (which positively impacted arcade games, as well), plus knock-off clones of already established and successful arcade hits, the dominance of the home video game console seemed poised to take over the electronic game market.

But a flood of clunky, low-quality games inundated store shelves, saturating the market with a plethora of generic and forgettable titles. Coupled with this oversaturation was the rise in popularity of personal computers, which offered gamers new avenues of entertainment with more sophisticated experiences, ultimately leading to an industry-wide video game recession. Later, to be called the video game crash of 1983, the recession brought the home console market to a screeching halt.

Lasting from 1983 into 1985, the crash rocked a booming video game industry and bankrupted several companies. Major retailers were left with warehouses filled with unsold inventory, and many smaller game developers and publishers were forced to close. At the time, Atari was the undisputed leader in the home console market, but owning the rights to manufacture game cartridges for the 2600 (effectively blocking out third-party developers), game development missteps, and rushing to the market much-anticipated games that would fall flat due to accelerated development timelines, they weren't impervious to the crash. Instead, they were annihilated by it, racking up nearly a half billion dollars in losses (over $1.5 billion in 2024 dollars). Atari was to be sold off by its parent company, Warner Communications. The fallout from the crash was profound and far-reaching. Confidence in the video game industry plummeted, leading to widespread skepticism among investors and consumers alike. The crash marked the end of an era and ushered in a period of uncertainty. Thankfully (as billions would come to find out), a former playing card company founded in 1889 had, in the 1970s, ventured out of paper and into electronics.

What if the video game industry stayed dead and never recovered? If Nintendo® remained a playing card company and never ventured into electronics, leading it to the console space in the late 1970s, where would the industry be today? What would it look like? I'm sure there would be some semblance of a gaming industry, but I don't think it would be as popular or as prolific as it is today without Nintendo's® leap of faith. Globally, there are over three billion gamers, and those numbers are not too far below half for female gamers.[1] Had Nintendo® not taken a massive gamble on restarting a dead in-home game console industry, maybe another company would have taken that leap, but one thing we do know is that Nintendo® laid the foundation.

---

[1] Exploding Topics. 'Number of Gamers.' Exploding Topics, n.d. Web. 9 February 2024.

The release of the *Donkey Kong* arcade game in 1981 was in response to Nintendo's® *Radar Scope* release in 1980. The *Radar Scope* release failed miserably and, in doing so, created a financial crisis for the subsidiary Nintendo® founded in North America, known as Nintendo of America. Compared to the cartridge, CD, and now the non-tangible downloadable content, arcade games occupied a space about the size of a refrigerator in so-called "cabinets." Being so large, unused inventory—like the ones from a failed arcade game—would leave a warehouse-sized glut of wood, particle board, plywood, plastic, display monitors, coin mechanisms, and speakers. Nintendo of America's president, Minoru Arakawa, turned to his father-in-law for help. Why his father-in-law? Because he was the president of Nintendo®.

Hiroshi Yamauchi agreed to send his son-in-law a new game. How would a new game help? A new game would allow the existing arcade cabinets to be repurposed. Instead of completely trashing the cabinets and all the metal, wood, glass, and plastic with them, the cabinet could have its hardware swapped out. With a fresh coat of paint and some new graphics, a new cabinet was born out of a want-to-be-forgotten mistake.

The salvage project was assigned to first-time video game designer Shigeru Miyamoto. Along with chief engineer Gunpei Yokoi, "they broke new ground by using graphics as a means of characterization, including cutscenes to advance the plot, and integrating multiple stages into the game-play."[2] *Donkey Kong* was a commercial success. Its success sent the industry off in a different direction. Nintendo® would dream up, design, create, and produce some of the most memorable and successful video games (and some of the genre's most lasting, loved, and indelible characters) in

---

[2] Wikipedia contributors. 'Donkey Kong (arcade game).' Wikipedia, The Free Encyclopedia. Wikipedia, The Free Encyclopedia, 23 January 2024, 05:48 UTC. Web. 9 February 2024.

the history of the video game industry.

The rolling out of the *Nintendo Entertainment System* (NES) and *Super Mario Bros.* in 1985 rescued the video game industry from the depths of despair, and it would have a lasting impact on a five-year-old boy who received an NES and a handful of games on Christmas Day 1986. It's hard to believe the NES would be manufactured for a decade before finally ceasing production in 1995. Nearly forty years after its release, its seminal mascot would star in the second highest-grossing film of 2023.

Often, failures have a way of creating something even better. Maybe we learn from our mistakes. Perhaps we learn from what didn't work and why so we can make our next innovation, product, design, or idea better than the last. The *Radar Scope* failure allowed for a rebirth of design and creation, a rethinking of what should make a game great or, at the very least, appealing to a broader audience, and a reimagining of the arcade game space, paving the way for the next iteration of something even bolder and better . . . one that would be played in our living room for decades to come.

Power On

Ready (Player One;)). Start.

Follow the frog down the hole . . .

My name is Ario. That's not my first name; we'll get to that later. Ario's my last name, and everyone calls me Ario . . . including you. I'm third-generation here. Where's here? Outside of Seattle, northeast of it, in a place called Redmond. It's 1984. As April wraps up, we're coming out of another wet and gray Pacific Northwest winter. We're approaching Easter. Eggs are something I enjoyed coloring when I was a kid, but I'm too old for that now. I loved finding them, but now that I'm older, I take much more joy in hiding them. If you saw me, I'd look like I'm in my early twenties, but I could be any age if that makes sense.

I got a job interview later today, and I'm nervous just

thinking about it. Palms are sweaty. I need to relax. I don't have much going on in my life. No girlfriend, that's for sure. Girls make me nervous. I like to read, listen to music, and play video games. I slip on the headphones of my Walkman, and reaching over to my tape tower, I blindly grab a cassette and pop it in. *Click* goes the tape, and *clack* goes the Walkman as I shut the carriage.

I don't know what this is. What band is this? What song is this? The tape's in my tower, so it's something I bought, or maybe Koji left it here some time ago before his parents divorced, and he moved into that condo with his mom and her new boyfriend. *Du, du, du, dah-da, du, doop,* the melody goes, whatever it is. It plays in my head, bouncing in and out, fading away and returning. I listen intently for a bit, trying to decipher what it is. It gets in my head and won't leave, and sometimes the tempo picks up when it gets near the end of the song, but I don't know, I don't know music. I let it fade into the background. Two fresh AAs, so I know I'm good for a while.

I want to fire up my Atari 2600, but I'd get lost in that and would definitely miss my interview. I love my Atari. There are a ton of home consoles out there, but, for me, none of them compare to the 2600. I was an arcade guy in the seventies, but being somewhat of a homebody, playing my favorites from the comfort and privacy of my living room works for me. I mean, I'm not a complete loner, but I can happily chill in my room for hours on end and get lost in a good game of *Space Invaders, Adventure*, or *Pitfall*. But not *E.T.* Great movie, but that game sucks. I can't figure out what the fuck to do. I was so excited to get that game for Christmas—the one before last. I mean, getting older, I don't care much for gifts anymore. I used to count down the days to Christmas when I was a kid, but now I'm more of a Thanksgiving fan because of the food, but if I can get my parents to grab me a game or two without spending my money, I'm all for it.

My parents usually get me a couple of gifts. Often, they default to cash for a portion of the gifts because it's the easiest thing to do. But with me getting older, gifts are really for nostalgic purposes. Every Christmas, as far back as I can remember, my mom would get me an ornament, the kind that goes on the Christmas tree. She told me when I was little, but not too little, still old enough to comprehend that they're for when I'm older and have my own family and my own Christmas tree. I don't think that'll ever happen. But every time I unwrapped the ornament box, I would make sure to look at it for a long second, smile, and directly say, "Thanks," to my mother, knowing she would appreciate it. Then I'd put the box down, never to see or touch it again.

I didn't know where they went; I figured my mom grabbed them and packed them away in a box for that time when I did have my own Christmas tree. My mom has so many boxes of stuff in the basement that I assume one of those boxes is filled with ornaments from Christmases past.

Back to *E.T.* What a travesty of a game. When I got it, I was so excited to call Louis to come over and check it out with me. We loved the movie; we had seen it countless times in the theater, so we just assumed the game would be great, too. See, I do have friends; I'm not a complete shut-in. I have a few friends at least, some closer than others (Louis is my closest friend; he's like a brother to me. We actually look quite similar, though he's a bit taller and leaner, and most of the time, he can jump higher than me). We weren't really nerds, but we definitely weren't jocks, and we didn't hang with the popular crowd, either. We were just kind of there, getting by in school, hoping not to be noticed and most likely picked on. So, you didn't ever really want to stand out in a good or bad way.

It was the arcade that brought us together, but now it's an in-home console that keeps us that way. Louis—I called him by his given name the first day we met but never did again—from there on out, he was always "Louie" to me.

For the most part, my friends and I called each other by our last names, but it didn't work with Louie Grochocinski. No one could figure out whether part of his last name was silent. Do we omit the 'oc' part so that we pronounce it "Gra-chin-ski?" Even Louie pronounced it both ways, so we all just went with my appointed nickname of "Louie."

His teachers didn't even give his last name its due. If we got in trouble in class, it was always, "Mister Ario . . . ," or "Mr. Porter . . . ,"* etc., but for him, it was always, "Mister Louis . . . ." Eventually, his moniker got the first letter of his surname attached to it. Not by me. We don't know how or by whom. But I liked the sound of it, so I ran with it. Try saying it out loud.

Oh yeah, back to *E.T.*, it's funny how I keep forgetting to address that. Maybe I fell into another pit. I can still hear E.T.'s footsteps in my head as he traipses around an aimless green environment. I am pretty adept at playing video games, but this was tough and weird. I just didn't care for the controls. I know I could have learned and gotten comfortable with them over time, but it wasn't worth it.

We still had the classics that we loved, but weirdly, it's like *E.T.* killed the buzz around video games. I mean, it didn't make sense to me that *one* poorly conceived game could destroy an entire industry, but it did. *E.T.* had potential, but it felt so rushed to me. What a shock to the system the whole thing was. With this game in particular, it felt like the developers just phoned it in and went home . . . or maybe they went home first and then phoned it in. We've come so far since the days of *Tennis for Two*. A fellow gamer nerd, Jimmy Hecker, said they dumped all the unsold *E.T.* games in a desert somewhere. I think he's lying, though. I wish someone *would* take all the *E.T.* games and throw them into a landfill.

I need to relax before my job interview. I fall into my bean bag chair, and with a little shimmy of my ass and an

*I don't know how it came about, but we'd use the term "saucy" to describe Matt Porter's occasional classroom antics.

arch of my back, I get it just right. I told you I love video games, but books are where it's at for me when it comes to relaxing. I can't relax with video games; they're too intense. There's a goal to accomplish, and I have to be the one to do it: a line of aliens to wipe out, a magical chalice that needs to be returned to the golden castle, a pit to swing over en route to tap dancing on a crocodile's clenched jaw so I can cross a pond. If an obstacle stood in my way, I needed to blast it, slash it, grab it, roll it, hold it, fold it, shoot it, boot it, clear it, not fear it, knock it down, stack it up, smack it around or jack it off. . . . Wait a second, not the last one. Sorry, I got caught up in the flow of things (except for the obstacle of finding the three interplanetary telephone pieces in *E.T.*; I just ignored that one). I digress

Oh yeah, books. I like the classics. Given the year, you might guess *1984*; it's one of my favorites, but it's not what I'm reading now. No, Winston didn't get shot at the end—no need to kill a man when he's already dead inside. The book I'm reading is *The Great Gatsby* by F. Scott Fitzgerald. I find my dog-eared page and focus on the text. My eyelids are starting to get heavy . . . .

If I ever have a daughter, I think I would name her after his wife is the last thought in my head before I drift off to sleep.

EHHH! EHHH! EHHH! EHHH! The ear-piercing, head-splitting wail of my alarm clock rips through my body, jolting me awake as I jump out of my chair, *The Great Gatsby* tumbles to the floor. "Shit!" I yell. "I'm gonna be late for my interview." Frantic and a bit disoriented, I realize I need my keys. Keys. Keys. Where are my keys? I pat my pockets for the telltale bulge (not the good kind), but they're not there. With my frustration mounting, my frantic search grows more desperate by the minute. Our neighbor has a spare key, Saul. Oh, man, he's out of town, though. But that won't do me any

any good because he has a copy of our house key; I need my car keys. I'm not thinking clearly. I start rummaging through drawers, and every conceivable nook and cranny, but my elusive keys remain hidden. Maybe I left them in my car.

I hurry to the service door of my garage. It's locked. That's odd . . . and above the handle isn't the usual knob to turn a deadbolt, either; instead, it's a slot for a key. I'm locked in my own house. I can't go anywhere without my keys, let alone this interview. Each passing second amplifies my sense of urgency, like a timer ticking away towards zero and a "game over" for me and this interview. I pause for a second to take a beat and to collect my thoughts. Whenever I can't find something, my mom, without fail, annoyingly says, "retrace your steps." Fine, I guess I'll do that.

When I got home last night, I made a detour to the kitchen because I was hungry for some leftover pizza. Snatching a Coke from the fridge, I headed upstairs to my room. Typically, I leave my keys in my jeans pocket, but occasionally, I'll toss them in the bowl atop my nightstand (not that type of bowl—that one's hidden—I mean an actual bowl for holding random stuff). Surely, they must be there. Racing upstairs, I whip around the corner and burst into my bedroom. With the blinds drawn, my room is dim, but the bowl perched on my nightstand emits a faint glow inviting me to check it out. Fuck, no keys in the bowl, only a handful of playing cards in its place. Retrieving them: a jack, queen, king, joker, and ace, I uncover my keys . . . inside the bowl—literally inside the bowl, as if they were made as part of the bowl itself. No time to ponder the unexplainable.

The bowl bursts into a dozen pieces. Is that the doorbell? . . . As it breaks, instead of the typical crashing of glass, a delicate, high-pitched tinkling sound fills the air, almost like a hidden secret was revealed. Keys obtained!

I fly down the stairs past the front room (my grandma, who was born and raised on the south side of Chicago in the "backa-da-yards" neighborhood, pronounces it "frunch room"), heading towards the service door to the garage. I quickly flip over the deadbolt knob unlocking the door . . . I step into the darkness.

Level 1

Darkness no longer, as my feet step on the impeccably clean concrete floor of my car's home, my arrival automatically triggers the fluorescent tubes lining the ceiling to turn on. After a few flickers of light, the bulbs are now at full wattage. Their slight hum signals a charge in the air of quiet anticipation of what is to come. The glow of the overhead lights shines down like spotlights on a stage. And the star of the show—a masterpiece of engineering and design whose lines flow with elegance and aggression that speak of speed even in stillness—is my 328 Twin Turbo . . . my cherry-red chariot that will ride me into battle. After a moment's pause, appreciating its serene beauty, I remembered why I was here. I throw open the door and hastily slide into her bucket seat. The well-worn and slightly cracked leather isn't a sign of age; it's a sign of experience. Each crease and imperfection tell the story of countless exhilarating drives . . . and I know she's got one more episode to write.

I give a quick rub to my little F1 Machine toy car dangling from the rear-view mirror to bring me good luck.

The freshly waxed red paint job pairs beautifully with the black leather seat faces and a two-toned gray dashboard, door panels, and interior. The custom-designed after-market steering wheel I installed is shaped like the letter D, with the letter's hump pointing up. I look left, then right to check my side mirrors, then down at the dash. One key to unlock the vehicle, another for the ignition. I select the thin metal blade with the rubber-coated base before the teeth, gripping it tightly between my thumb and index finger. I prime her with a gentle pump of the accelerator, and then, with a turn of the key, she fires up with no hesitation.

The two big red circles on the dash always stand out to me: two -ometers, speed- on the left and a tach- on the right. I'm wired and ready to go. I throw the floor shifter in reverse and peel out of the garage. My garage is painted sky blue to match my house, and the whole thing's topped with a gray roof. My neighbors to my left and right have brick houses with black roofs.

"Fuck!" I yell. While backing out, I nearly hit a kid on his bike. I know who he is. Man, that kid is something, hauling ass on his bike, slinging *The Daily Sun* into my mailbox without fail Monday through Sunday. Maybe he's so good because there's a training course at the end of my street. I've never seen it, but I guess it's there. Oh, and I don't know the whole story, but I think he once stopped a thief, too. What a true hero.

I live on a vibrant street. I walk down it, and I have to dodge radio-controlled cars, that punk skateboarded kid, and another asshole breakdancing on the sidewalk. I think he's breakdancing, though it looks like he's badly injured and has possibly lost movement in his upper body, and only his legs can flail about. He looks like a turtle stuck supine on its shell. Maybe he needs help. Shit, I feel bad now.

I recall one time strolling down the street, and a goddamn tire took my ass out. Did I trip over it? Nope. That fucker was rolling down a driveway and took out my legs.

And that was shortly after I dodged a lawn jockey running across my path. Is the village ever going to get that section of sidewalk fixed? And why do some of my neighbors have headstones in their front yards? Did you bury your relatives under your front lawn? Weirdos.

I saw the Grim Reaper once—it must've been Halloween, but that doesn't feel right. It doesn't make sense that I get my paper delivered, but a stack of tied-up newspapers is also sitting on my driveway; I don't get it. *The Daily Sun* has got to get their shit together. That doesn't seem like a wise business practice.

Get this: when the paperboy finishes his route, he comes across random dudes sitting in the park cheering him on. For one, that's weird, but they didn't even arrive together, either. They're each sitting separately from one another, so I assumed they showed up on their own. It does NOT feel right, for sure. Those dudes have got to be child molesters. I worry that kid is going to disappear one day. Now that I think about it, I live on a bizarre street, but I have no time to worry about him or that. I have got to haul ass to this interview.

Man, it's a beautiful, sunny day out here. I throw on my blue and red shades to dampen the sun's intense glare. Palm trees line the foreground of the horizon, and a sparkling crystal blue ocean backs those palms before meeting a rich blue sky peppered with clouds. I start on Sunset Boulevard with one goal in mind. To keep me on track, I have checkpoints in my head that I must reach by a specific time. I slam the gas, and the engine rips with a blend of beefy muscle and high-pitched air intake, kicking up a cloud of dust in my wake.

I push the RPMs to the max, redlining at 158 mph. I don't know if I should go this fast with this number of curves on Sunset, but I have to get there quickly. I'm dodging bugs along the way. Everyone in town has the same car and one of two colors, so my cherry-red 328 Twin Turbo really stands out when I'm blowing past everyone. A plethora of street signs line the road, but they're of no use because I can't even read them at my speed.

I'm cruising along and making great time. The purr of the ponies is lulling me into a state of ease, but suddenly, I'm slapped back to reality. A flash of olive drab from an out-of-control military jeep careens into my lane, cutting me off. I began shouting, "Hey, you jacka—" luckily avoiding me, but before I could get out my complete tirade of insults, the car next to me was T-boned. POW! The jeep slammed into the turquoise hatchback, completely obliterating it. Squinting into my side view mirror, I see what remains—not much. Err! What a 'deyyyck' that driver was . . . makes your blood boil when people drive like that. Good luck to them, but I don't want to be a witness to that accident; I have somewhere to be.

A bright day quickly grows dark without even really a dusk period. The sky is an ominous black but lightens up as I approach the San Francisco Highway. I see the big city ahead of me, and some new styles of cars join me on the highway. Now, it's nighttime. The new rides and I trade a little paint, but nothing too severe, and there's nothing to derail my progress as I make it to Grand Canyon Avenue, passing my favorite grease joint, "Ruins of Athens Gyros," along the way.

I flip through the radio channels, but only three come in. I must be in a dead zone. Distracted by the thoughts of delicious gyros in my belly, I lose focus and get cut off by a lime green coupe. It's like the drivers are trying to force me off the road. There was no blinker as it changed lanes, either. I slam on the brakes and downshift, and with the speed dropping like a rock, the RPMs shoot up. I can't avoid limey; I ram right into the back of him. The back end of his car acts like a ramp for mine, which sends the 328 airborne. Flipping over, I land on the roof with enough force to bounce me back upright. Amazingly, the car doesn't show a scratch, but the whiplash knocks me out. The last thing I recall is hearing DJ Jenny on Resistance Radio, 120.48 on the dial. She can be a bit of a snob, but I like her. If we ever meet, she would see I'm pretty classy.

Level 2

Is this heaven? Am I having an out[er] of body experience? I'm In the sky. Am I dead? Wait a second, I'm falling, not rising. Fuck, I wasn't that bad in my life. Man, I'm dropping quickly races through my head once I've had a minute to process what's happening. Whoosh! I feel a sudden gust of wind hit me. I'm yanked up by my chest and armpits. The cold chill of the wind rushing into my face slows, but now I realize it more. I'm starting to come to my senses. Where the hell am I?

The sky is blood red, and I see nothing but jungle below. I assume the plane I was dropped from is the one trailing off in the distance. I gather my bearings enough to grab the straps of whatever this harness is still riding up my armpits. I look up, squinting as the light reflects off something. I'm attached to a parachute. I've never skydived before! Holy shit! I have to land this, or I'm going to break both fucking legs.

I pull it off. I don't know how, but I land, and my chute is gone, too; in its place is a pack of smokes. Man, I'm rank. I don't know why I smell so bad. I'm on a peninsula of a dirt path surrounded by thick brush, trees, and jungle on three sides. I can't get through that stuff, so I guess I'll take the path. I have to get out of here. It's night now, but it's hot and muggy; the coolness from dropping out of the sky has worn off, and I feel bugs on my skin, including one buzzing in my ear. I see some stars in the sky, and one big star stands out. Goddamn, what's this buzzing in my ear? That's not a bug; what the hell!?!

"Jeff Grande with an 'e,' but the 'e' is silent. Listen up, soldier," he commands. That's an odd way to introduce yourself. He's my boss, wait, what? I'm on my way to an interview; how do I have a boss already? I'm trying to get a boss. A 'grey' fox scurries across my path—it looks lost. I'm getting sleepy; I feel asleep if that makes sense, but I must push on. I progress to a truck after being chased by a pack of Dobermans. I sneak up on a lone wolf and clip him with a couple of right jabs. Let the rest of your pack know I mean business . . . yeah, I'll punch a dog!

I find another couple of trucks and hop in to find some new swag. Uh-oh, the truck have started to move. Man, this is a rough ride; where am I going now? I find a gas mask, and I hear Jeff Grande in my ear. He tells me to use the gas mask in gas-filled areas. How did this guy ascend to boss status? It must be the Peter Principal. I hear from Jeff again, and he has a mission for me. Finally, some direction, and now I can get out of this place. He warns me, "not to let enemy detect you." Jeff's not one for definite articles, I guess. Then, get this: he tells me I can change floors using the elevator and to remember their locations. How is this guy my boss again?

Sweet, I find a gun, a Beretta M92F, let's have some fun . . . with no bullets . . . aaaannnndddd here's Jeff right on cue to tell me to find some ammunition for the gun. I mean, this guy has got upper management written all over him. Did Schneider fart in here? Then, the boss chimes in about the gas mask again. Oh yeah, well, he provided some value there. In addition to that one Doberman, some fools eat a couple of right jabs as I make my way through the compound, dodging a giant ass rolling pin along the way. Let me just scan my key card to get through this door. Nope. How about this one? OK. Let's try this one. Alright, the fourth time's a charm.

I'm told to talk to Diane because she can help me, but, of course, she's out shopping. I found myself falling out of the sky into the middle of the jungle, then roaming around some military compound, and Diane's out shopping. Women, am I right? Oh look, first a gun, then missiles, got some food in there, too, and now I get to carry a cardboard box. Gee, thanks, Jeff. But this place will teach me how to use a grenade launcher, so it isn't all bad. I find out the cardboard box comes in handy a time or two. And guess what: when I find some ammo, all I have to do is call Jeff on the transceiver, and when I end the call, there's more ammo again, right in the same spot. It works for food, too.

Striving to get around undetected has ramped up the anxiety-induced sweat even more than when I landed. I'm even more rank now than before. Shit! I'm captured. "Under arrest!?!" I exclaim. What for—punching that dog? I think to myself. I can't believe this; I'm stuck inside a door-less room, four walls with only four barred windows to let in a little light. How'd I get in here, and more importantly, how do I get out? Did they drop me from the ceiling? It's starting to sink in that I'm trapped and beginning to grow stir-crazy. This isn't good, this isn't good. I'm getting anxious and claustrophobic. I feel this nervous energy building up inside of me. I start pacing around, trying to figure out what to do. I call the boss, and he proudly boasts, "Mission acc-omplished." What? Wait, so getting my ass locked up was my first job here. I still don't understand how I have a boss. Apparently, I have a job, too, but I never made it to the interview. I have got to get out of here. I feel my heartbeat racing and heavy bullets of sweat streaming down my forehead. My palms are sweaty.

I can't take this anymore. Flying into a fit of rage, I wildly start throwing punches. Aimlessly, I'm swinging at anything and everything. In doing so, I don't realize how close I'm getting to the wall. Shit! That hurt. What the fuck!?! "I punched the wall so hard I opened a door?" I confusingly said out loud. Ahh, fuck, with the adrenaline wearing off, the pain in my hand is quickly setting in. Now my hand is killing me. When I get a chance, I have to see Dr. Pettrovich (the real one) and have it checked out. Hopefully, his receptionist, Ellen, will be in the office that day; she's cute . . . and I think she's into some kinky stuff, too.

I wonder if Jeff is giving it to me straight or if this is all just a big boss lie supplying me with false information to carry out some maniacal plan. As I approach the door, I'm cautious about what I will walk into. Stepping into the darkness, I duck, but I'm no coward. I push forward . . . to the left, not to the center, and not to the right. That was a close call. It's all over, at last. Is it?

One final buzz in my ear, a new waveband: 120.77. Time to meet my creator(s).

Level 3

Ding, ding, ding. I snap to it. I'm confused and disoriented. It's bright, and the roar of the crowd starts to seep into my brain. My palms are sweaty . . . as is my whole body. Beads of sweat dot my forehead and face, dripping into my eyes. The salt creates a mild stingy sensation, so I try to wipe my eyes. In doing so, I hit myself with a rubber pad. What the hell, I'm wearing gloves?

Boxing gloves. They're green in color—oddly, they're only green when I box, but white when I'm at rest—matching my shorts. In noticing my hands, I realize my right hand still hurts, but now my left does, too. After blinking to clear the sweat from my eyes, I notice an older guy beside me on the other side of the ropes. I'm standing in the corner, and he's right next to me. Leaning over the ropes, he's close enough to my ear to be heard over the crowd, but before he speaks, I muster, "I want to see Dr. Pettrovich. Are you him?" I slow my delivery on 'Are you him?' knowing full well he's not.

"Yeah, yeah . . . I'm Doc," the bug-eyed man with a towel around his neck barks into my ear, his fist pumping without stopping. "Stick and move, stick and move!" he shouts.

"What!?!" I exclaim. I don't know what that means.

But I have a bad feeling he's not going to explain it to me, instead, I'm just going to have to figure this out on my own.

"I'm your trainer, but don't get any ideas like those other guys cornering—freaking weird! Sure, they got better boxing techniques, but there are just some things as a trainer I WON'T do . . . not anymore, at least!" With a squeeze of water into my mouth and a slap on the back, Doc sends me out of the relative safety of my corner.

I have no clue what he's referring to, but fuck it, I guess I'm a boxer now, I tell myself, hoping that it steels me for what I'm about to do. I gotta do what I gotta do to survive out here. I need to plan something fast, a little machination if you will. 'Round, 'round, 'round, I go. I have a lot of heart, I tell you; maybe I can be a star, but I'm a zero right now. I start punching. I'm little, so I have to jump every time I do it. I don't know much about boxing, but I don't think this is the best form. This joeker across from me with the glassy look in his eyes is as scared as I am. That protruding chin makes for a nice target, though. Oh yeah, 'stick and move,' I recall. Punch and dodge, punch, and don't get hit.

I deliver a fury of punches to this bum's jaw, dislodging a wad of spit each time. He keeps taking 'em and taking 'em and taking 'em. I pop him with a couple of right hooks, and he's seeing stars now. I throw a couple of body shots just to change it up—I don't need to jump for those. He finally peels back to avoid my assault. Did this motherfucker just say 'c'mon,' and give me the 'bring it' hand gesture? Oooo, I'm going to dance like a fly and bite like a mosquito all over your ass now! I think that's the saying. Anyway, I got some ass to kick. He approaches me, looking to close the distance, and one well-placed punch to the kisser floors him. This is easy. I'm a natural. "Stay down!" I taunted him. Oh, you want some more? Let me start you off with one of these. I rare back, wind up and deliver a massive right uppercut to this bum's face, and down he goes a second time. This is too easy. Man, he *still* wants more. OK, no problem.

Holy shit, who the hell just got up? He's twice the size of the last guy, and what's with the 'hey you' eyebrows sent my direction? This guy's relentless; he's got a motor on him like a Honda. I'm going to play a little defense and dodge his punches—dodge, dodge, counter punch, dodge, dodge, counter punch. Wait a second, he's got a tell. Those big, bushy eyebrows flash every time he's going to throw a punch. Oh, damn, he released a combo of punches I wasn't anticipating. I'm hit, but I gather my senses, and I'm back. I've never been punched before, but I shake off the shock and return to my plan—watch the eyebrows. I slip in punches where I can and dodge his telegraphed ones. I can tell he's wearing down. I keep unloading on him. Jabs, hooks, and power punches are doing the trick, and I finally drop him. My God, his feet are huge. I mean, they're literally the size of the referee. It's over, ladies and gentlemen!

Ahh, it's time to relax in my pink jumpsuit and savor my big victory. "Wait a second, your fat ass is gonna get on a bike, and I have run behind it!?!" Doc stares blankly at me. This guy never blinks, and he's still pumping his fist at me. "Training, what do I gotta train for? I'm the champ, baby!"

"Well, you can't just stand there like a statue, lady; you can't take liberties with this game," he fires back. "If you can do this, maybe I'll give you a pass."

"Word," I reply.

"Listen, kid, that's the only slack I'm gonna give ya. I gotta keep ya off the streets; these broads are bad news."

"Why? What? Who?"

"Women."

"What's the problem with women?"

"WOMEN . . . WEAKEN . . . LEGS!!!"

" . . . " He sounded so old and raspy at the moment.

There's a minor problem here that's about to become something more significant. I got more boxing to do, sir. Cut to the next fight. . . .

Look at this guy entering the ring with a flower in his mouth. I dance all over him, hitting him with alternating left and right shots to the grill. I make easy work of him.

Open up, fat boy! I got a knuckle sandwich for you. X marks the spot. I pop this guy so hard I knock his pants off. Enough shots to the belly, and he drops. He's unable to get up. You've got to be joking; maybe he broke his hipp, oh, that would be a bad way to go out.

Oh great. This guy's wearing a skinned tiger for a robe. I'm handling him pretty well, and he's got a tell, too. Holy shit, he just disappeared on me. Where the fuck is he? *Bap, bap, bap,* I eat three punches before I can even comprehend what's going on. I'm getting peppered with a flurry of punches, and he won't let up. I'm done. For the first time ever, I kiss the canvas.

"One . . . two . . . three." I hear the rhythmic counting of the ref rattle around my brain. This guy was like a great magician out there; I was charmed by his punches. I pull it together and stagger to my feet. I'll be ready if he tries that disappearing act again. *Ding*. I'm saved by the bell (I'm so excited . . . I'm so scared). It's been no fun club today, that's for sure.

Holy shit! Who's the giant bald man charging at me!?! What was once a constant and noble approach to this game has turned my adversary into an instant bull in the ring. With a full head of steam, he bounds forward at me. The last time I faced an unorthodox move, I went down before knowing what happened. I'm a major boxer now, sir, cuz I'm going to stand up to him, face his charge, and watch as I deliver a well-placed shot to his belly.

My shots are getting stronger, to the point where

every punch I land to my opponent's face sends his eyes spinning like the reel of a slot machine. After a well-earned break, it's time to cool down with a soda pop.

"HAH-HAH-HAH."

What's that noise? Who's there? I'm getting tired; I turn pink with lethargy to match my pinko stinko opponent. *Ding*. I'm still exhausted. Maybe I need some steak or a lovely Spanish rosé to boost my energy. What should I select? Doc's never-ending pumping fist pumps faster now. I feel rejuvenated, but the guy across from me wants to put me to sleep. My star is brighter now; I'll start him with a power punch. Man, he has quick hands and combos, but he telegraphs his punches. Did you know the first 800 phone number was 800-422-2602? But if you called it, it was always a busy signal. It's simple: I need to dodge his punch and then counterpunch.

Oh, super, another macho man of a fighter. He's got a real Hollywood look to him. Palms are sweaty. I hit him with a hard right, sending him flying into the corner belt buckle. And a hard left shoots him to the other corner. He can flex his pecs, but he's dizzied now. I find the key to winning this fight. With no help from the cameraman, the bearded man, or the bespectacled man, I'm on my own. Palms are sweaty. This is a story of true victory.

BOOM! In a flash, I'm down, like a stick of dynamite went off, kid. A muffled cheer rattles around my consciousness. Is that a Bronx cheer? A silhouette hangs over me, crumpled in a ball I lay . . . I guess my fingers just weren't fast enough.

I mutter, "Mister, are you a dream? I tried to keep it clean."

Level 4

The silhouette over me extends a hand and helps me up. “Hell yeah, nice stop, player!” he emphatically tells me. The glint of his earring catches my eye. We must have had their same play called, a run to the left off tackle, and we stopped that for no gain. Now, a run to the right up the middle into the heart of our defense. We bottled it up, no problem, bringing up third and long. It must be a passing down for them. “Pass! Pass!” the leader of our defense yells. Even though the game has already started, it’s another coin flip. Tails never fails, and they went heads because their speedster receiver goes streaking down the field past our flat-footed defensive backs. Giving chase, we pull him down well past the first down marker and deep into our territory. It’s a big gain for them and a fresh set of downs.

They started their first drive of the game with a sweep to the left, so we played for that tendency and called our corresponding defense. It’s a run; we guessed that right, but, boy, we don’t know everything. This one’s to the right between the center and guard who have our nose tackle and end engaged. Ordinarily, this goes for a significant gain, but our monster of an outside linebacker reads the play and comes crashing down the line to make the tackle, holding the runner to a gain of only a few yards.

It's second and long, and we play for a pass. Our line quickly collapses the pocket, and we sack the quarterback. We had that play figured out from the get-go. It's a huge third down here. This team's built for the run, so we play for that again. An ankle-grabbing tackle from our safety saves a touchdown, and he manages to drag down the runner short of the line of gain.

It's fourth down, and we hold them to a field goal attempt. The long snapper whips the ball back to the placeholder, and the guy who helped me up a minute ago comes firing through the line, unblocked (how did no one account for *him*?). He dives for the holder, not even allowing for them to get the kick off. The field goal attempt is blocked. It's like they didn't even try to block him, or maybe they couldn't stop him.

We're on offense now, and I must be a two-way player because I'm out there blocking. Tangled with the defender, we scrum and fight for position and leverage. I lose. I'm launched, getting some serious air; I must have been thrown five yards easily. I'm tossed about like a rag doll, banging my head as I bounce off the turf . . .

Level 5

The room is spinning. Wait . . . I'm spinning. *Poof. Poof. Poof.* I just let a couple rip . . . bombs, that is. The explosion of the blasts gives me an extra boost, propelling me to new heights as I unfurl in the process. This could be useful since I imagine I can't jump too high in a metal suit. The suit consists of long, slender gold plates that protect me, and it's adorned with a red breastplate and topped with a red helmet, plus red boots to match. My vision is tinted as I see everything through a green visor. Uniquely, the suit has a very curvy design, almost effeminate in its appearance. But the more I move, the more I realize this suit offers me amazing abilities. The right arm of my suit is a cannon; I can shoot, but oddly, the projectile unleashed from my hand cannon doesn't travel far before disappearing.

I stare up at a seemingly endless shaft lined with gold, but plenty of spikey crawlers and flying lobsters stand in my way. As I zoom through it, I just start blasting; some enemies are killed while others are unaffected . . . what a ripp-off. Some of the ones I kill leave behind little purple dots that boost my energy.

Holy shit! Something just dropped from the ceiling on me. I get hit and took a bit of damage, and then the thing just exploded. But I keep blasting away because I never seem to run out of ammo. Goddamn, there's shit coming out of the sewers at me, too. Maybe in a different world, I could enter these pipes . . . what a warped thought.

I continue blasting, ducking, jumping, and dropping into a ball when needed. I kill some flying bastard that had its sights set on me, and it leaves behind an energy bump for me, but I can't get to it. In my onslaught of aliens, I notice the unclaimed energy bump hovering above the sewer blocks other baddies from coming out after me. Hmm, I can use this to my advantage.

I come across a red door, and my usual blaster won't do the trick, so I select to give these missiles a try. It's a long shot, but it works! High-five! But nobody other than this statue is around to give me one, and his hands are affixed low . . . err, low-five it is, is what I chose. Oh, I'm just going to curl up in a ball, perch myself on this statue's open palms, and take a little respite, too, where no one can see me.

I'm back at it, blasting my way through this planet. I get stronger along the way by picking up energy tanks and more missiles. What I thought would be a mellow time through an uncharted territory has been met with a river of flying creatures with spastic wings, giant sharp talons (or do you spell it with two 'Ls'?) dive-bombing me from above.

I'm running out of ideas. When in doubt, I just start laying bombs. I blast away a chunk of the floor over a pit of yellow . . . something: lava, acid, piss; I don't know. Welp, this suit should protect me from something, so I trust my instincts and drop down. It worked—nnnnn-ice! I continue. In my aimless blasting, I knock a hole in the ceiling. I'm starting to realize how to navigate this foreign world. As I stare up at the ceiling to figure out how to get up there, it regenerates, so I shoot the ceiling again. Then it dawns on me: when faced with a barrier, I cannot waver in my determination, and I need to take a variance to my approach to traversing this planet. Soon, I'll learn it's a method that suits me well. I can jump up there, and if I time it just right, I can use the respawned ceiling as a step. Let's do it.

Fucking shit! I'm stuck in the ceiling!

Like everything here, I blast my way out. Palms are sweaty. Goddammit! I went through a door, and some fucker followed me to the next room, hitting me in the process when I transitioned between rooms, unable to defend myself.

I get stronger by picking up energy tanks and more missiles. Sweet, an elevator. Will this get me out of here? Umm, I can only go down deeper into this hell hole of a planet. Holy shit! Dragons just popped out of the lava and shot fire at me—these mo-fos buried, flop over them to obtain a power-up.

More baddies, stronger ones, too. Screw 'em, I jump and spin right through them, attacking in the process. Another elevator, and deeper I go. Aww, sweet. A random energy tank is lying on the floor. I don't have to work for this one; it *could* be too good to be true, but fuck it, I'm so excited, I'll just run full speed after it. GODDAMMIT! I knew it. I recover and find my way back to grab the energy tank, carefully jumping right before where I fell last time.

Now face to face with a purple pterodactyl alien-looking hybrid, it lofts some fireballs my way. I freeze them. From my boxing days, I learned to close the distance when faced with a bigger opponent. I stand right next to it while it loops fireballs over my head. Safely out of harm's way, I blast away, never relenting; it of this world, I rid, leaving a bunch of missiles for my efforts.

I find myself in another battle with a new foe. This one is more challenging than the last. In a pool surrounded by acid, this squat fellow features formidable defenses. He slings boomerangs from his back and shoots spikes from his front. A near-constant barrage of projectiles from him leaves little opening for me to attack. Perched up high, I see a chance, so I drop down and rip off a couple of missiles, then back to my high ground to wait for another opening. Fuck it! This is taking too long, I'm going in. Thinking back, raiding his nest with a ball and bomb approach could be foolish. Yeah, I take some damage, but I deal enough to blow him up.

Shooting statues of my recently slain foes reveals a pathway to a never been explored portion of this planet. This must be the way out. Great, another elevator down. Palms are sweaty. HOLY SHIT! A jellyfish with giant fangs darts over and latches on the life of me to rob; I'd give in never, for I've come too far. I curl up in a ball and bomb the shit out of it. That can't happen again. Another one locks on to my movement, and with one well-placed shot from my hand cannon, I put it on ice. That's my only approach with these bastards: freeze and move.

Materializing out of thin air, little rings target me. Oh! Is that spaghetti? Probably not. Oh, if they were, I would cheer. I must be getting close. A barrier of something stands in my way. I can't tell if it's an organic material or not. Though surrounded by glass, I can't crack or break it. I put a few more missiles into it to shrink it, but I get knocked off the platform. In my attempt to get back up, the barrier regenerates, costing me more missiles to destroy it. It must be alive to heal itself like that.

I'm getting peppered from all angles, losing energy, and burning through missiles. Palms are sweaty. It's like time is slowing down. I clear a few more barriers. There she is . . . the mother of all enemies. I, on this mother with aplomb, rain down all hell. Encased in protective glass, the first missile opens a hole and exposes her tender flesh. She's eating missiles left and right. While trained on her and unaware of my surroundings, I'm hit and knocked into the lava. I regained my ground to unleash another onslaught of missiles. Shaking ferociously, I can tell she's badly wounded.

In her death, one last 'fuck you' to me—she initiated a self-destruct; a time bomb was set. I need to get out fast!

There is only one way to go: up. I jump and jump and jump. Some platforms are large, and I easily land on them, but others are only as wide as my boot. Palms are sweaty. I contort my body mid-jump, doubling back to reach a platform. It's tricky, but I have to move quickly. With no time to think, I must rely on my instincts.

I leap but misjudge my approach. I clip my helmet on a platform above me, throwing off my angle. Shit! I'm falling. Fast. Left, right, left, right, I move my body, trying to grasp the tiniest footing of a platform, any platform. In my fall, I'm thinking about all the ground lost from my ascent and how I'll need to make it up. I catch sight of the rapidly approaching floor—the same floor where I began my climb out of this nightmare of a planet. I tightly close my eyes, clenching my jaw and grinding my teeth as I brace for the inevitable impact. With the anticipation of the impending crash: this just in, bail? Eyeing a chance to start over pass as words through my mind.

Level 6

Crashing down to the floor, I land. Of course, my suit protects me. But wait—my suit? It's changed; it's different now. It's blue—light blue with dark blue gloves, boots, helmet . . . and a speedo. It's an odd design choice. Contrary to pictures of me holding a pistol, my suit still features a built-in hand cannon. And my visor is gone, too. Oddly, every time I jump, I need to open my mouth.

OHHH, FUCK! My disembodied head is lying on the ground. That's fucking scary. I'm not going anywhere near that. Some guy tries dropping bombs on me, but I make quick work of him. Toothy-smiled green beanies are swooping in, trying to hit me, but they're no match for my mouth-agape jump-and-shoot approach.

I've got guts, man! Bombs away. I progress through blasting what resembles an erecting metal phallus, shooting white projectiles at me. Ehh, gross. A jumping robot hits me, and it hurts—easy there, big guy. I dash under him and blast away. A couple of block throws cut deep, and my opponent is quickly sliced and diced.

There's so much action going on that I feel time is slowing down and I'm sluggish. What a charge this stage has been! I bolt up the ladder and gash my next opponent with two well-placed slashes. Sliding on ice, I fall into the water, astonishingly, without making a splash. I find myself in a large, empty room with no way to escape. Fortunately, some random blocks appear; they aid my ascent, but they're extremely tough to cross. If I ever do this again, I hope it's easier. It's been a wily goose chase thus far. Will it continue? But I have no fire to melt the ice, man.

Level 7

All I needed was my flying skills. I launch. Altitude and speed rise quickly; I'm amongst the clouds. Quickly, bandits fill my radar and conveniently fly right into my line of sight. These enemies are dangerous and foolish . . . I might be worse, but you want me on your side. I make quick work of them with my wing-mounted rapid-fire barrel machine guns unleashing great balls of fire. Hounded by enemies, I rip off a few missiles, dodging counterfire in the process . . . quantity over quality. A bird joins my starboard side. Hey, tiger. Hell, I'd take some help up here, but you're too slow for me. The chopper drops out of sight. Midway through my run, a flash of lightning rips through the sky. Is that a Russian attacking me? I heed its warning and lock on to it, but he acts easy to my presence, so I know he's an ally. That devil barrel rolls out of sight. Only an ace can fly like that in that old thing. In my earpiece, I hear, "Captain, look over there in the sky; a hawk has joined us." I didn't know they could fly that high.

Fuel low. Speed up! Speed up! Speed up! Left! Left! Right! Right! Down! Down! Connected. Technology is amazing: not only can I refuel mid-air, but I can also reload missiles. Danger! Bogey on my tail, let's turn and burn. Hard left, hard right, hard left, hard right, I lose him. I don't have time to think up here; if I think, I'm dead. Palms are sweaty. Hair on fire, flying by the seat of my pants, no one can predict my next move. Don't "Easy there, tiger," me; I'm a one-man wolf pack. It's been a wild goose chase up here, not a walk in the park for this free spirit. I could tell you more, but it's classified, and then I'd have to kill you. Time to land this bird, but first it's time to buzz the tower, and I'm not sorry about it because I feel the need, the need . . . for speed. Don't tell me this isn't a good idea; and I'm not a problem because my ego's writing checks it *can* cash, son.

Altitude is dropping quickly. Speed leveling out, but it's too low. Up! Up! Speed Up! Up! Up!

"I'M TRYING TO GO UP!!!" I shout.

Speed Up! Up! Up! Speed Up! Speed increasing . . . shit! Too high now!

Speed Down! Left! Left! Speed Down! Right! Right! Speed dropping, but dammit, now it's too low! Up! Up! Speed Up! Up! Up!

"I'M TRYING TO GO UP!!!" I exasperatingly yell in a defeated tone.

Speed Up! Up! Up! Speed Up!

"I'M COMIN' IN HOT!!!" . . . . I'm a ghost.

Level 8

Returning to my haunt. My Castle. My home.
In the highest keep, I sit on my throne.
They killed my wife, so I created a world of evil.
They excused what they did, but *I* caused a major upheaval.

Only one family rang the bell,
to mount the charge into my hell.
I shall sic on them my vile forces
to inflict harm, and punishment my curse is.

Under a blood moon, my hunter approaches.
With whip in hand, his fate he imposes.
In my clock tower, he rides gears and crosses.
All along slaying my henchman and bosses.

Owls hidden in the shadows, bright glowing eyes.
Sacrificing their own, spiders descend from the skies.
Skeletons can't die, only crumble to a heap.
Fire-breathing bone pillars earn their keep.

Hunchbacked gremlins erratic in their movements.
Stalking mummies reanimated by an evil spirit.
Cyclops charges forward, swinging a hammer his desire.
Men engulfed in flames, blaze ground in a wake of fire.

Quick release of a dagger, ghosts from a distance stagger.
Dosed with the acrid water holy, enemies are slaughtered slowly.
With a looping axe, an armored knight puts up little fight.
Fire and ice from a companion freed, my minions abandon and concede.

In a graveyard, a pile of bones resurrected.
A doctor's monster no longer seeks affection.
Two fire-breathing dragons spew forth flame.
A demonic bone dragon, chased away, now in frame.

A half-breed child, my hunter's adversary.
In defeat an offer to align, now matters vary.
My flesh and blood, half human, half me . . .
I gave you my name—it, you rearranged.
Traitor, how can this be?

I am the Dark Lord. Who darkens my door?
I'm twice your size, blue face with piercing eyes.
Bolts of flame arise as I lift my sceptre to the sky.
Teleporting across the room, your end is nigh.

My many faces of death: stalking, taunting.
Oozing blood from my orifice: gawking, haunting.
Ungodly winged beast, true form revealed, energy bolts my defense.
One final whip, disappearance, my death hath commence?

Will I return a century hence?

In my extended slumber, a grand son returns.
Mine? Yours? It is left to discern.
Greeting him, my outspread cape releases a blast that burns.
But the Evil Count's impending doom is of no concern.

Him cowering in the corner, I can't attack, by design.
His bravery and boldness, with my scheming, now combine.
One final whip makes my demise, part of a larger plan
to place a curse upon him and his clan.

"What a horrible night to have a curse."
Ghosts and ghouls go from bad to worse.
To the safety of their abodes, the townsfolk disperse,
replaced by zombies who boast intentions most perverse.

"The morning sun has vanquished the horrible night."
The crack of the Vampire Killer, a sound to its handler's
delight.
Acrid water holy burns bright, secrets made clear.
With a strike of the stake, a symbol of evil will appaer.

A crystal bought white, bartered for blue then red.
,Kneel to view ways that otherwise mislead.
Hidden books provide secrets and clues to be read.
Aromatic leaves allow passage through lakes of dead.

"Garlic in the graveyard summons a stranger."
A requested gypsy offers a knife.
Garlic in the mansion presents a danger.
A requested gypsy gifts a bag of life.

Invest in an oak stake?
I shield you with my rib to take.
Invest in an oak stake.
My heart, passage the ferryman will make.

Invest in an oak stake.
See with my eye through walls fake.
Invest in an oak stake.
The strength of my nail gives power to break.

Power to make evil burn awake
is offered kneeling by the lake.
Invest in an oak stake.
A disembodied face sheds tears of ache.

A golden dagger freezing in its wake.
In defeat, a magic cross for your sake.
Steal my ring, entrance to my castle?
Your access, I cannot forsake.

A desolate path upon which my assassin snakes.
Rib, heart, eyeball, nail, and ring bakes.
Now, the Prince of Darkness awakes!
With flame so sacred, a formidable foe I do not make.

With skies red, the earth shall tremble and shake.
With skies clear, sense the text does not make.
With skies gray, wounds prove fate, lacking haste, my killer's mistake.
For now, I rest; for now, I break . . .

A ghost [lying in wait]

Level 9

. . . in the graveyard. It's dangerous to go alone. Fortunately, I took this with me [I slash with my sword—*shh-woo*—a projectile firing from its tip]. I didn't start with the sword; I found it. Despite visual proof to the contrary, I did not have another option.

Going up, left, down, and left again (I'm not lost) has led me through the woods to here. I'm hesitant to lean on a gravestone, for it might release a ghost, but I've learned something could be hidden below. I find something magical, but I don't have enough 'heart' to master it (which wasn't a problem with the last sword offered to me). I do have heart . . . but I know courage won't come until next time.

I set out to prove my worth, hyped to rule this land, to be its hero. Is that a donkey with swords for arms? Fuck! I take an arrow to the back. I touch a knight statue, and it comes to life. Not thanking me for bringing life to it, instead, it tries to kill me. Bombing walls and burning bushes proves that property destruction has its advantages. Sometimes, I find secrets to everybody, a game of chance, or angry cave dwellers who charge me to repair their broken door. Word of advice: if you ever find an old man who offers you either a life potion or a heart . . . always take the heart.

I'm just trying to climb stairs here, and a falling boulder violently crashes towards me. Unable to move laterally on the stairs, I'm hemmed in, and backtracking my climb is my only option to avoid the boulder of death . . . it didn't work. I stop, watch the enemies' movements as I clock their habits, but frozen in time, they make for easy kills. Dungeons with snakes, bats, blobs, and skeletons are no match for my trusty sword and shield. Speaking of skeletons, they're not good at hiding items. Materializing from the wall, I try dodging a giant hand, but I'm trapped and taken back to the start. I must be getting close to something.

I return to where I was taken away and make quick work of a fire-breathing dragon. I link up with the old man again; he hands me a letter to fill my heart with love [potion]. I bargain shop for a bigger shield—boy, this is really expensive! But I shop around to find the cheapest price possible. Arrows aren't cheap, either. I have to save up money for a ring. No, not for a princess, for me. I blue almost all my money finally buying it.

Palms are sweaty. I come across a horned beast. "You don't want none of this smoke," I warn him as I strategically place bombs in his path. He gobbles them up and is quickly defeated. I battle on, finding good fortune (plus a raft) in one auspicious shaped dungeon. My new raft floats me away.

I make use of my boomerang to pick up far away items, but not too far away. The enemies are growing stronger. I'm progressing, but I need a break . . . but I won't die . . . so I back up and, in a second, control myself enough to recharge my batteries. Rested, I'm back.

"Ahhhhh, shit, give me that back!" Something ate my new big shield . . . at least he was kind enough to spit out my old one. Like, like, why did you have to steal my shield? Note to self: every time I come across a single block, push it. I lean against a statue to rest; of course, it comes to life, but it's not all bad. I pair a bracelet with my ring, and I can feel its strength. Now you're playing with power, I say to myself.

I dodge some bouncing, mice-like creatures. I try yelling at them, but I'm not loud enough to scare them away, so I slash instead. Maybe I should whistle at them . . . I find a flute; I blow into it. Its airy sound is recorded for posterity. With all my might, I obtain the power to unlock any door. Crossing rivers of blood, I come across a giant spider, and a couple of well-placed arrows to the eye slay him. I'm told a secret, nay, a fairy good secret, about where they don't live.

Grumble, grumble . . . goes my stomach. I'm hungry, so I grab some grub but find a better use for it. Another fire-breathing dragon, another dragon slayed. The enemies grow more numerous and become very difficult, especially when found in areas with projectile-shooting statues that can't be killed.

Another dragon, this time with more heads, is slayed. My heart is full, as is my head with battle-hardened wisdom. I enter death—dark thoughts, I know—but I'm no shadow of myself (that will come in my next adventure . . . and I won't cower in the corner, though that confidence might make for an error, I'll have company). Will I make a spectacle of myself remains to be seen? I encounter my most formidable foe yet; one I must patranize repeatedly, so I map out a plan of attack. I ready myself with a new ring. A rrow of silver lines my quiver.

I can hear the beast a room over, eye must be getting close. I come face to face with a giant pig-like creature. Palms are sweaty. The battle begins. I try to force with power my sword into him, but his disappearing act makes it a more formidable challenge. I stun him with a few slashes. Now's my chance to ennd him, to end <u>this</u> quest. With my eyes fiercely fixed upon my adversary, I reach over my shoulder into my quiver. Gently but with a purpose, my fingertips graze the coarse bristles of the fletching. Careful not to disrupt their alignment at the risk of altering their accuracy, I lower my hand to grasp the shaft of one silver-tipped arrow. This arrow must fly true. Removing it from my quiver, I nock the arrow in one fluid motion. Eagerly anticipating the familiar feeling of the string's tension, I draw back my bow . . .

Level 10

And fire an arrow at a grim-looking man, hoping to reap some hearts, but he sees me and freaks out, siccing his minions on me. Nonetheless, I cash in.

An evil snake woman has pitted me against a slew of enemies to free a lady pal untenable to me. I harp on the fact that I can play a tune to turn my enemies into mallets. Being selective with my shots is a skill.

I have a nose to find a chamber a different route would have hidden; in it (although with large hearts), bespectacled flying foes have bad intentions. In my quest for the three sacred treasures, I drink from the floating chalice of life when I feel low. From left to right / right to left I go to make my climb. I pay to play a treasure game, winning a single feather. Huh?

I try intimidating the storekeeper. I'm no angel even in this land (but really, I am), but I can't win because I'm not strong enough; I go on. I barrel my way through, not losing my bottle for life, but in my haste, I fall off a platform from where I just jumped. Fortunately, I'm light as a feather . . .

"I'm Finished," I am not. Now I know its use.

A group of four flying eyeballs dive at me; I duck, avoiding them, then fire upon their half-hearted attempt to hit me. Winged nuisances fall from above; they recoil at the sight of my arrow and soon become hissstory. I played another treasure game and, to my credit, came away with a nice prize. After enduring training, it was such an outstanding performance that I took a (sacred) bow. I'm no weakling; look how much farther I can shoot. Another chamber: I'm skilled enough to take what made him glad I came.

I embark on a fortress. I select a mallet and sober up some stoned archers. An empty hospital is of no use to me. I drop down from a platform and come to a room filled with eggplant-launching wizards—didn't expect to see that here. I move on.

I come to a room with a pit of yellow . . . something: lava, acid, piss; I don't know. Déjà vu . . . as to why: hard solving for an ace detective, let alone me. This seems familiar to me, in fact, elements of this world and some of its enemies I think I've seen before. I had good luck last time I dove into a pit of yellow, so here I go again. Hot damn! I spring up with renewed health.

A two-headed beast stands between me and a much-needed treasure. One final arrow for t' win, and the beast bellows in pain. Pinchers shoot up from the ground, and while I avoid getting hit initially, I can't duck in time to avoid its spat projectile.

A bounding thief comes for my hard-earned possession. My bow is useless against him, so I stay grounded and slide under his jump, avoiding his sticky fingers. A snowman launches snowballs at me while I'm elevated above him. I drop down to the next platform and melt him with my fire arrows.

I precariously jump from ice cap to ice cap. Night has fallen. I briefly grazed some lava, but I was quick enough not to take any damage (surprisingly, water instantly kills me), nor was the lava's heat intense enough to make me melt.

I come across another fortress. I get whacked with an eggplant, and now I'm cursed with an eggplant for a head. I blindly stumble to a hospital where a kind nurse produces a remedy. I find a map, I check it, but it's useless; pencil me in for torching this thing the first chance I get.

Another boss, another battle, a giant snake-like monster, but only one head this time. Arrows firing, by my mighty darts, the beast hewn, draw back my bow, and I release one last volley. I treasure the ability to make light work with my arrows. To the sky, I go.

Amongst the clouds, I jump through them and land; I'm light enough to prance on them without falling through. A familiar enemy, a jellyfish appearance with sharp penetrating fangs, dives at me. I have bad memories of these but can't place where and why. I battle on to the largest fortress yet.

As I slay the final beast, a blob-like creature, I don't know what box I've opened. Him, with arrows I peg, as suspected, wings I receive. I fly, and I fly, and I fly, but I fall. A dilemma deduced sadly by me because I'm far from the sun, but I'm still a son, never to be an adult . . . I am a forgotten hero.

Level 11

Falling, I somersault into the sweltering jungle.

Up I stand, shirtless, rippling muscles, rifle in hand, headband taut across my forehead; my rifle becomes a machine gun.
Up I look, a much-needed shotgun power-up.
Down, I lie prone to avoid enemy fire.
Down, I drop to gain a better vantage point to blast the locked door.
Left, I dart across the screen, avoiding a bomb tossed my way; I lay waste to a couple of foot soldiers.
Right away, I'm in a boss battle; flashing lights make it easy to find my target.
Left to my own devices, I ascend a waterfall, blasting through soldiers and fixed machine guns.
Right arm whipping of an alien head, its mouth agape spitting fire at me while it guards another entrance, but I eliminate it by blasting it with a pummeling barrage of bullets; my jungle fight is taken to the snowfield and back in base again.

Blazing flame bursts impede my progress, but my skilled timing avoids getting me torched.
A giant bionic man with spiked shoulders won't let me pass, so I lay into him with repeated bursts of my heavy shotgun; his jumping over me makes for a perfect target, and he meets his demise.
Startled by an alien scurrying quickly towards me, I kill it and soon come upon the alien's heart.

Destroyed the vile red falcon and saved the universe;
consider yourself a hero, I'm told (now, I am recognized) . . .
I escape.

Knifing through the atmosphere.
On top, I hug the left and find a sweet spot to avoid the double volcanoes spitting fire in my direction.
Nestled between some rock formations, I'm like a vicious viper waiting to strike when the enemy appears.
Adding an extra turret to my ship, I've doubled my firepower.
Missiles released tracing the contours of the topography they find their targets.
In search of power-ups, I blast everything in my way and uncover what I need.
Cornered under a hail of gunfire, I dash my ship to the right to avoid the barrage, slipping past untouched.
Once again, my nemesis . . . a big core belief of mine is to fire upon anything impeding my progress, but this time it's different; with my finger off the trigger, I dodge and move, slipping between its beams.
Dodging giant ring shooting statues, all head no body, I head east—err, is landing this ship an option or what?
Efficiently, I make quick work of a squadron of ships, baiting them up and down; I'd love to open fire, but I must show restraint, "mother . . . !" and I chill, drawing from my past to stick and move.

Gradiually, I use my shield; as it turns red, its protection decreases, and I'm vulnerable.
Ready for another barrage of intergalactic space invaders, I tighten my grip [palms are sweaty].
Activation of another shield couldn't have come at a better time as I prepare for another battle.
Dueling with an aimlessly floating chunk of space flesh as its whipping tentacles fire small bullets in my direction while I unleash hell on its pink fleshy center, shriveling up its existence.
I'm pegged down by space debris blocking my path; I unleash a trifecta of lasers, slicing right through it to clear a path.
Undeterred, I switch off the laser and opt for the double shot so I can better canvas the tunnels.
Shoot ahead with my ship, slip by the closing lock, don't mind me and I won't be bothered by you (have we met before?) . . . a life forced from salvation meanders across space and time; I was the first, not t*he*y who came before me.

Final Level / Boss Battle

Duh nuh nuh nuh nun na.

Finally, I have made it to my destination! It's quite an estate they have here. There were many obstacles along the way (what an adventure) that were overcome by me . . . and by you, bil-leeee-v-me [said in my best Louisiana Creole drawl], but we made it. In the foreground, a towering piece of artwork commands my attention. An intricate design showcases a collection of shapes, patterns, and blocks . . . but it is a design that feels unfinished, like a puzzle missing its final piece. The artwork unveils differing collections of cool or warm colors depending on the sunlight's reflection. Built of only four distinct shapes: straight, square, L, and zigzag, they combine into an interlocking quartet rising from the earth, but its ascent does so cautiously, as if mindful not to rise too high. After pondering its existence and trying to figure out what it is and why it is here, I have concluded: so be it; a mind game it is.

It's hot out here, like a desert (odd for the Pacific Northwest). The sun is angry today, my friends. I've heard of the man on the moon, but if I squint, I can almost see the scowl on the sun's face. To my left is a dreamscape of a garden abundant with sprouts, turnips, onions, beets, radishes . . . and a cherry tree (a unique pairing amongst a crop of root vegetables). At the cherry tree for five seconds, I intently stare, manifesting its reason for being there, when I spot a giant frog hopping towards a thick hedgerow of tall grass with a solitary tree in the distance. His entrance is thwarted by a dog patrolling the area. At the foot of the tall grass, a basset hound sniffs around. Nose down, butt up, tail excitedly wagging as he shoots around the clay ground. Suddenly, he leaps into the tall brush—he must have caught a scent of something—his big floppy black ears perking up as he jumps. Disappearing from my view, he startles up a couple of ducks moments later. One with a green head casually flies away, while a purple-headed one frantically darts to and fro.

I see another duck; he's purple as well, but he's different. He's a lot more animated, and his wings are a darker shade. Or is that a cape? He looks at me and puts his finger up to his beak [wait, he has hands?] and tells me to S.H.U.S.H. I suspect something F.O.W.L. is going on here . . . or maybe it's just gas I smell. A couple of heavy claps of thunder appear rowdy enough to provide cover for him to vanish into the shadows. With his disappearance, I now notice another flock of feathered tales amidst the tall, thick grass . . . or possibly sugarcane. But scroo(ge) it, that's enough bird stories, although I would like to tell you how cute each one is with his color-matched cap complementing his outfit.

As I continue down the path, I stumble upon a collection of bikes piled near each other. Biking to work is common, but dirt bikes seem like an odd choice for transportation. A plume of smoke rises from one—looks like it over-heated. Two cute little critters scurry across my path (one a bit chipper than the other). I nearly stepped on them; one hid under a box that acted as a shield, the other just backpedaled. Fortunately, I caught myself in time to alter my step so they wouldn't need rescuing from the stomping of my Ranger boots. They scamper off. No longer surprised by their presence, I can now discern their outfits: the black-nosed one looks like a famous adventurer, while the red-nosed one resembles a detective or more like a private investigator.

Maybe that's what chased them away: lurking in a sorta nook, I see a raccoon. Suited better for raiding garbage than scaring away cute critters, this trash panda makes eye contact with me and freezes like a statue. He thinks I have him cornered, but I just want to get past him. He senses danger from me, but not to be upstaged, he furiously whips his tail about enough to elevate himself off the ground. Is that play for him? Will his path to exit stay just right for him to escape and for me to continue walking? I break my stare with the raccoon when I see an overgrown man-child topless in a grass skirt hurrying towards me, his feet moving a mile a minute. I wonder where that boy—err—man is off to? Ah crap, he just made eye contact with me, and I can tell he wants my help.

"Master," he begins (he's close enough upon me now that I notice a milk mustache), "which dock ta sail from?" Showing me a letter in his palm (a fistful of fruit in the other), "Dis prints es teeny."

I don't know how to answer him. To a warmer ocean climate is a venture I land on in my mind's list of possibilities to where he could be going. This is not a conversation in which I want to engage, so I keep moving . . . but I can't stop thinking about that letter. Maybe it had a hidden message on it he needed, or maybe what he was looking for was written in the stars. In the tropics, where I've decided he's going, is where he'll find it. That reminds me of when my archaeologist uncle, Steve, sent me a letter (a stained letter, actually) from a long voyage in the islands. He was in the water—probably why I could tell the letter got wet before—on a boat, or maybe it was a sub. See—yo, yo, I'm talking to you here, pay attention!—if I have to go somewhere far, I'm taking a plane—something big—like a 747.

And now, coming my way is a skinny, bearded man in red skivvies hoisting a lance high above his head (are there more of him, I ponder). My thought shifts to go stand 'n go blend somewhere into the background to avoid getting impaled. I keep moving.

Minding my own business, I abruptly get sucked over to my left, the gust of air pulling me in enough to lift me off the ground for a split second. As I drop, my left foot instinctively braces against the curb enough to give me a bit of traction to regain my footing and sprint away from whatever that was. Sensing that I'm out of harm's way, I look back to see a puffy pink thing with rosy cheeks (Is he blushing? Maybe he's embarrassed?), his mouth wide open, attempting again to suck me in. I can see that he ate bits of little animals, but, fortunately, I'm too big and now too far from his breath's reach.

A set of stairs before me, I watch two turtles descend, one up near the top and another before it. Giving the turtles their right of way, I pass a flagpole as I approach the entrance. The façade is covered in ivy or maybe vines, some shooting so high into the sky that it's as if they could reach the clouds.

Off in the distance, I catch a glimpse of a meteorite shooting across the sky, but my eyes become fixed on a welcome sign posted before the door. It greets me: WARNING!! TRESPASSERS WILL BE HORRIBLY MUTILATED. I think about my situation for a second and what brought me here, "Should this man shun this interview?" Reasons are many . . . "Ack," I say out loud with contempt for that sign. That's a crazy way to greet a potential new hire, but I'm at this point and [clicking is the sound made by the door handle as I turn it] I'm not trespassing. They wanted me here . . . they need me here.

But then I stop. Before entering, I step back a few feet from the main door to get a better angle of sight. Over to the right, around the corner, I see two brothers, twins: one toe-headed, the other chestnut, getting ready to duke it out with some high school kids. But these kids mean business. They're ruthless. Equipped with brass knuckles and lead pipes, they come out swinging. One brother throws an oil barrel, and the other pulls out a whip. One kid counters by launching a trash can while his buddy stones his foe with fast hands. On the foe's chin, a small river of blood comes to sit; teeth gritted, he ran some interference knowing he had to take one for the team (what a slick move). BOOM! A small stick of dynamite explodes, distracting the punks, allowing the blonde-haired one to grasp a head full of jet-black hair from the nearest one and repeatedly dish some violent knees to the face.

[I haven't seen fighting like this since that hockey game I attended. And that was in the stands, not on the ice, when some knucklehead with a switchblade steeling beers from other fans incited a brawl.]

The thrashing was so hard that he dropped his lunch money while the blast's concussion elicited a barf response from the other. The blast was so jarring that a tiny-footed bystander practicing martial arts is waddling off like he just shat his pants . . . behind him, a trail of bees gives chase. In his hand, the pants portion of his sleeveless white (well, no longer) karate gi is klung. Fun times.

"Hey buddy," a bleached-blonde kid in a tailored suit yaps at me, "you wanna get a little action in on this?" Smacking a rolled-up newspaper against his palm, he's leaning against the wall. Streetwise, I am not, so gambling with a stranger is not my thing. He pushes off from the wall and starts pacing around. Appearing agitated, he's back on the wall again, but uncomfortably so, and he begins tapping his foot incessantly. Unaware, he knocks over his briefcase.

"You interested in buyin' a boat? What about a girlfriend? You want mine? She's a bit of a prima donna, but you can't put a price on love, or can you? I think you can *precisely* put a price on love. What will ya offer? I bet you don't know I own a castle. Have you met my uncle, Mr. Benedict?"

"Uhhhh, no thanks," is all I could muster to his varying off-the-wall questions. He's sniffling a lot. Maybe he has a cold.

"I got a hot stock tip for ya. Have you seen my barometer around here? You think we're heading for a recession? Should I short Yapple? No matter what, do not . . . waste your time . . . with the carnival." Slowing down his delivery for once, he must be serious about this carnival thing.

"No, I haven't, and thanks for the tip."

"But I didn't give you the tip . . . only Pris likes the tip —hey-hey!"

"Uhhhh, no, about the carnival."

"You goin' to the carnival? I'll go with ya, let me grab 'sila, we'll double date. Are we taking my Fairrari or yours? I just wrecked my 328, had to get a new one. Good idea, I'll drive. I can tell you about the time me and Billy Ray Cupid shorted the shit outta frozen OJ futures. We really nuked 'em, those Duke brothers!" he proudly boasts, but I have no clue what he's talking about. I'm sensing a theme here. "Hey, you like to party?" he says to me at a volume that amounts to a stage whisper.

"Umm, sorry, I gotta run, man. I got places to be."

"Right-O. Dude likes to par-tay, alllll righhhhht," he excitedly says while nodding his head, a big grin on his face. "Use it . . . or lose it," he shouts as he disappears around the corner. I don't know what that means, but I don't care because I'm just glad he's gone.

Back to the fight.

With a fist full of shirt, one brother yells, "Tell me what I need to know!"

"The password? Haaaa! That's your fatal step; it's thirty-two characters long . . . but smiles are free." And that's what he got: a big toothy grin.

Unsatisfied with the answer, the brawl continues—double trouble from these two pairs . . . but in a back alley, not on a half pipe (the place must not have been able to get a permit to build one). Hoping to skate on by to not get dragged into this fracas, I decided I better move along now. What was once trouble on the double, drag on no longer will this fight, because suddenly everyone is distracted.

"By George," I mutter out loud to myself. "What is that thing?" My awe-struck gaze moved higher and higher to find up the ramp a giant ape-like creature. He starts smashing a building with his bare hands. What kind of vitamins has this guy been taking? Maybe he's part of the demolition crew, and they're remodeling. Out of the corner of my eye, I notice some armed green men behaving like teenagers, each with a bandana colored bright—not muted—in-to an open sewer hole they ninmbly jam and turn 'til they're out of sight. Cowering, a bunch gone. Meanwhile, other green men hop on hoverbikes and speed off, avoiding barriers along the way (well, trying to, at least, but they're not too successful at it).

Suddenly, a flash of purple draws my attention away from the giant ape. With his sword sheathed and ready at the hip, a man bounces through the alley, spin-jumping onto a sign several feet above his head. He barely grazes it, and then in a flash, he's on top of the roof (knocking down a lantern in doing so . . . but I don't think it was accidental). I can't even process how one could move that fluidly. Staring at him in a confused state, we make eye contact.

"Walter?" he breathes, his voice muffled with an air of revenge about it.

"Hi ya, buh . . ." I trail off, "say . . . how did you get up there?" Befuddled, my inability to force out a coherent response is enough of an answer for him. With one more flip, he's out of sight.

I have finally reached the entrance of the red and white building that houses the game design company known as FAM. I, completely confounded by my path here, have exhausted myself from the quest. Now, a new one lies before me, but I'm here at 8:40, even a little bit before my meeting time. By my calculation, I have six minutes and forty seconds until the whole world is about to change, but it might happen a bit sooner . . . well, it must.

I can feel my pounding heart like a jackhammer slamming against my chest. Little beads of sweat dot my forehead, and I have a touch of swamp ass, too. I close my eyes briefly and take a long, slow, deep breath. I held it for a beat and then exhaled as slowly as I inhaled. Trying to steady my nerves through repeated breathing techniques only allows for a multitude of thoughts to race through my mind, each competing for my attention like my favorite Atari game begging to be played. With a final determined exhale, I open my eyes, straighten my posture, and run a clammy hand through my mop, trying to make whatever I have going on up there presentable. My hair is so tough to manage; should I have worn a hat?

I enter. Oh boy, a bowl of jellybeans perched on a small table is a welcoming touch. Next to it, a note reads: USE DIFFERENT FLAVORS TO . . . [blah blah blah—it's not worth the trouble]. I crane my neck and see an entrance to a kitchen—must be where this stuff comes from. With a shock of purple hair, a pajama-clad little boy—couldn't be much higher than my knee—moseys over to me. He is clutching a tiny car toy in his right hand. It must be his favorite because the micro racer is all beat up with not much sheen on it anymore. Half asleep, he mumbles, "Sir, real-ly, I dreams of candy." I toss a few beans his way.

"More, more, more . . . feed us." He's not making much sense. "My goal really is to find keys."

Switching subjects, I ask, "Hey, who's your buddy over there?" motioning to a similar-sized boy, but one who sports a more standard-colored head of hair. Searching for an answer, he seems a bit puzzled.

"Whatchamacalit . . . ultimately, Sam. Son's on some stuff, I'll tell ya that. Ya know, rich kid problems, split personality thing. He's a good kid, but best to leave him alone and forget about him."

Noted, I move on.

A large man in a purple tracksuit ominously stares at me. I think I had the same outfit but in hot pink and a much smaller size. For he's security. He's sitting down, slumped against the wall. A blank expression on his face. Is he dead? Nope, he's alive . . . very much alive! I don't know why, but I feel nepotism got him the job. He motions for me to take my sweater off. I oblige. Security, huh? Well, what for? I'm not going to R.O.B. the place. Hit with a hunger pang, or maybe it's just a pre-interview nervousness; I think how a gyro might hit the spot right about now. I should have stopped at "Ruins of Athens" on my way here; their food will stack-up against any grease joint in the area.

I'm a few steps into the building. I take a second to look around to get my bearings. A black-bearded man with horn-rimmed glasses to match clumsily charges forward in his brown trench coat [a flash of light] as he zaps past me. His pink trench coat, the color of bubble gum, and shoes pitter-pattering about as he bounds up and down my way to warn me, "Danger! Watch out for falling rocks." Confused, he's got my attention now, so he goes on. "Hey, got any of those black panther diamonds? What about some red balloons? I don't need ninety-nine of them—twenty will do. Have you seen King Dom? Any power drinks or roast chickens, huh?"

"I don't, pal," I spit out as he hastily trails off in his

green trench coat. Quit playing detective with me. A bottle whips across, nearly hitting me. I duck down to avoid it and find a floppy disk lying on the floor. I pick it up. As I analyze it, a hi-tech-looking ninja strides my way. "I'll take that, thank you very much," he says as he plucks the disc from my hand. The bottle, oh yeah, who threw that? I turn to my right to see who the culprit might be.

I espy two mischievous-looking characters snickering in the corner. I'm not well-versed in mischief, so this bottle-throwing nonsense I can't grasp why. Identical twins, I'm guessing. They have egg-shaped heads, exaggeratedly long pointy snouts, and large dark black eyes. The only difference between them is their outfits: one is dressed all in white, while the other is all in black. The only contrasting element is the band around each of their wide-brimmed hats, which matches his brother's color. Diabolical toothy grins can't mask their true intentions. They're up to no good. Would it be MAD of me to ask, "Who threw that bottle?" But I don't want to rag on them. Hmm, they're shaking hands now, and I can see each holding something behind his back. One a gun and the other a knife—who brings a knife to a gunfight? I think they're after each other . . . maybe I wasn't their target. I look elsewhere.

Off in the corner, beneath a dimly lit lamp, I see two battle-hardened veterans weary from their latest noble endeavors. One is a fighter, the other a warrior, settled in at an antique oak table, trading war stories. With wooden mugs filled with libations in hand, frothy ale sloshes over the side as their chronicling (however, one is far more versed at this) begins, deep into the knight they will go (well, at least one will). You can tell they've heard each other's tale a thousand times before, yet each will still deliver his own as if it were the original telling. The fighter, clad in bright red garb matching his red coiffure, and the warrior, protected by blue armor, lean in closer to each other to bend an ear. I still have a bit of time, and this conversation might be too good to pass up, so I hang around within earshot of their table, hoping to gather some good office gossip.

Blue begins, "Seeing you in the light, I can tell battle has aged you."

"Well, lucky for you, you haven't changed a bit," Red snipes. "I guess when you fight as much as me, it takes its toll on ya. Is fighting something you even do? Remember that time you ran from a slime?"

"He was metal! I couldn't kill him . . . and he ran from me, ya know! Least I wouldn't run from a pack of gray wolves; I fought wolves before with no issues."

"Pack!?!" Red shouts. "Dost thou mean wolf singular!?! Since when have you had to face multiple enemies with your mano a mano combat style?"

"It's not too hard facing multiple enemies when you've got a team with you: thieves, monks, multi-colored mages, ninjas . . ."

"Yeah, yeah, yeah, I get it," Red cuts Blue off. "At least you don't have to share the gold and XP."

"Remember you left your buddy stoned that one time, and he didn't get to *share* [eye roll] in any of your *hard-earned* XP?"

"Listen, you know who this goes; you and me both have got to be selective with our turn-based attack system. Say it with me now. R P G—"

"—R P G . . . thou hath maketh a fair point."

"Stop talking like that," demands Blue.

"You started it. Don't forget wizards, too; wizards on your team, pretty powerful."

"Oh yeah, wizards. I loaded them up with some spell they wanted—of course, it cost me. Nothing's free—well, plenty of free spells in your land—I asked them how's it goin'. I was advised to temper my expectations," Red snaps back.

"Hmm, purchasing magic must've been nice; I had to earn it . . . not free for me."

"Well, it must be nice to *earn* a heal spell right out of the gate. You know what happens when I need a heal potion? I have to buy one potion, and then buy one potion, and then . . . buy . . . one . . . potion. No buying in bulk in my land."

"Ooooh, dost thou wisheth thou shalt buyeth in bulk f'r his charm'd health elix'rs?" Blue sarcastically prods Red.

Red quips, "Alright, cool it with the fancy lad talk, Bill Shakespeare."

"Drinks on me tonight . . . and every night since, ya know, deeper pockets and all," Blue proudly boasts.

"Yeah, don't remind me of the chest of gold that never disappeared only to magically replenish itself."

A fresh set of mugs arrive.

"I thank thee," Red flippantly responds.

Red lifts his mug up high, taking a moment to bring the conversation back to center: "Whether it be experience points, levels, new weapons and armor, whatever, one thing we can both agree on is nobody, and I mean *nobody,* grinds . . . like us." Mugs collide; fortunately, they're wood, not glass. Some foamy ale bubbles over the side, trickling down the mugs across their knuckles, splashing on the table.

A large gulp of drink allows Blue to offer a moment of reflection. Blue speaks thoughtfully, "Yeah, we're not that much different after all: both had to rescue the king's daughter; both fought wolves, wyverns, dragons, and ghosts [simultaneously, they both sing, "I ain't afraid of no ghost."]; I was chasing a Ball of Light; you were after a crystal . . ."

"Well, four crystals to be exact, but who's counting . . . lucky you not to deal with Warmech—AKA *Death Machine*—either, or that annoying *EHHH* noise when someone got poisoned."

[Wait, I've heard that noise before, but there's no time to dwell on it as this tête-à-tête continues.]

Undeterred, Blue continues, "My point is, we both started from nothing, built ourselves up into something amazing, and in the end, we saved our respective lands and turned out to be pretty popular because of it. So, I propose a toa—"

Red butts in, "Well . . . yeah, but, I mean, you got pretty popular after that magazine giveaway though."

"If I've told you once, I've told you a thousand times, I was on a quest in a foreign land. That was going great. I came over here, and I have to change the name to avoid infringing on a trademark, so I lost a little goodwill that way, but I'm sure there'll be a sequel if you know what I mean. Nothing *final* about what I'm doing, and, who knows, maybe I'll give that quest a go again."

For once, Red is speechless, but not for long. "Final, huh? Yeah, I don't think so. Trust me, in time, I'm gonna be far too big for this land."

"Eh, maybe, we'll see if you have any sort of legacy. Speaking of legacy, let's not forget . . ." Blue points a thumb at himself, "Descendant of the great Erdrick—the man who created a rainbow—am I not, and I do wear his armor pretty well to boot?"

"Did I ever tell you about that little cemetery in that little town of Elfheim? The tombstone reads: HERE LIES ERDRICK. You would think such a great man would have a bit better burial place, no?"

"Nope, I know that tombstone, it reads: HERE LIES LINK. No idea who that is, but that's not the great hero from the past himself. Maybe this Link character is a hero elsewhere, but not in Alefgard."

Like always, a moment of respect, contempt, hatred, and jealousy sinks in for both. I can tell it has happened countless times before, and I know it'll happen countless times again.

A bleary-eyed Blue says, "Thy night is getting long in thy tooth, dost thou wisheth to retire to our respective inns?" Muttering under his breath with purposefully chosen words, yet still loud enough to be heard by Red, "Or maybe you could pitch a tent?"

"Well, at least my tent allows me to save my progress. Oh, excuse me, I mean," an air of pretentiousness lay thick in his voice now. "Will thou tell me now of the deeds, so they won't be forgotten? Thy deeds have been recorded on the Imperial Scrolls of Honor."

"Yeah, yeah, yeah, he's a king. Would you expect anything else?" Blue sloughs it off.

Red, trying to bring tonight's tall tales back to him, says, "Did I ever tell you of my battle with the evil King of the Dark Elves?"

"Is that the one where you switched alignment with a party member so that he got rubbed instead of you?"

"It's called strategy—[ah-hem]—I mean teamwork. When you have clinics that revive people, why not sacrifice a party member?" Red realizes his choice of words was not the most careful, but it's too late to walk it back now. Red clears his throat, "So . . . uh . . . where was I, umm, Astos, the Spell Caster . . ."

"Ass toast, the smell caster? What type of story is this?" Blue needles Red.

"Forget it; *you* don't get to hear how I got the Matoya Crystal."

"Right, right, and then it was used to get something to [Blue using air quotes] wake the sleeping prince. I think we all know how the [even more exaggerated air quotes now] wake a sleeping prince story goes."

Agitated, Red fires off, "Prin*cess*, sleeping princess, that's how *that* story goes . . . big difference. Well, I'm off . . . boarding my airship to Gaia." Red plops his mug down on the table.

"You have an airship!" Blue blurts out before he can even think of suppressing his jealousy, but drink makes for loose lips, and his incredulous response is telling.

"Yep . . . and a boat . . . and a canoe. Enjoy footin' it all over Alefgard, pal."

As Red pushes back from the table, slightly stumbling to grab his footing, he's met by Blue's retort, "Gaia, huh? Good luck with that. That place is alllll an illusion . . . as for me-eth surely dost thou wonder. I'm off to Rimulder . . . to get some puff-puff!" A dejected Blue, bothered by his contemporary's swift exit, announces his evening's festivities to anyone who would care. But the only one who would, was already out the door. Reflectively he utters, "Maybe I should have stood with him." But who is 'him?' I know it's not Red.

While a rich hero, I pity him, but I'm distracted when a young ladd, blanketed in lime green, flashes before me. Grappling with what I'm seeing, I come to understand he has a mechanical arm (that's pretty rad, I think), which allows him to swing by (on his command, originally) any albatros encumbering his progress. He tells me (but it comes off more like a warning), "A master plan, diabolical in its intentions, a plan so badd. Me, like a ton of bricks it hit, learned, have I to resurrect a man so vile, it must be killt. You've got to get out of this base, for it will explod in sixty seconds." Judging by his wild, fiery red hairdo, I think he might be a bit crazy.

A bit frazzled and with no suggestion as to where to go for my interview, I push deeper into the building, passing some burning oil barrels (what an odd choice to heat the place) and a broken ladder along the way. Before me, a bunch of guys dressed in black suits with matching fedoras. They were not interested in me, though, as they popped in and out of rooms and hopped on and off doorless elevators (don't let OSHA know about those). There's a lot of action here; it's a busy place. Maybe they're looking for someone else? I hear a loud bang—was that a gunshot?—then glass breaking as something comes crashing down. The lights go out momentarily but are back on a few seconds later. Among a collection of purple doors, a single red one stands out to me. This must be where I go.

As I approach the red door, a group of goons ease too close to me for my liking. I back off, giving them their space; I can see that they're just kids. I guess they can't be up to too much trouble; I'll give them the benefit of the doubt. Unlike most kids I know who move at a snail's pace—or is it a sloth's pace?—these kids are frantically moving about. Then they start excessively knocking on every wall, floor, and ceiling imaginable. One pulls out a hammer (while the fat one pulls out a candy bar)—maybe rooting for a bit of civility amongst teenagers is too much to ask—he's not going to use that thing, is he? Sizing up his swing, he closes one eye—will he do what I think he's going to do—BAM! The hammer bashes through the floorboards with one quick strike, creating a large hole. I take back my 'can't be up to too much trouble' comment. They all circle around the newly formed hole and peer into it. With a leap, one by one, I watch them go into the fray—tell each one to be careful, I wish I could. That never-say-die attitude can get you into some sticky situations sometimes. I'll give them their time down there. That's not my place, so I head for the door. As it closes behind me, I faintly hear, "Heyyy . . . youuu . . . guyyyyyys!"

I stepped into a new room. Though expansive in size, I'm struck by how overcrowded it is. Its frenetic atmosphere is intense and intimidating. Unlike any color scheme I've seen before, it's a matte black room with a less-than-lustrous gold finish (distinct from the shiny gold finishes I've seen elsewhere). Are all of these, umm, people here for the same position? Well, 'people' might be a loose term. I see a mix of ghosts, demons, grunts, and more. Walls and barriers—some displaying cracks—in every direction create a labyrinth-like office space, I suppose. I don't know where to go. As a group of ghosts scuttles past me, I instinctively take a step back to avoid their charge, inadvertently crushing a pile of skulls and bones. The ghosts start to disappear, one by one, until finally, a figure—a human figure—emerges. His vibrant green attire immediately catches my eye, and his archer's cap boasts a single prominent red plume jutting out of its fold. I can tell he was a bit dandy-looking before, but all his speeding about has made him wiry and a bit gaunt. "Let me let you in on a secret," he says. "He who is the fastest gets the spoils. For the stage, it you must conquest or perish."

"Umm, OK, but how do I get out of here? I need to get to my interview. Time's running out."

"Ahh, I get it, just like those treasure rooms. Well, that's simple: just shoot your way through until you find an exit door and hope it's not the one that takes you back to the start," he replied with a smirk. "Don't worry, you'll get there . . . eventually." Still holding his smirk, he followed it up with a wink.

That doesn't sound promising. "Well, alright, thanks."

"I assume you can shoot diagonally, right? Not like that pussy, Thor!" A hearty laugh erupts as he sprints off. *Errr-ruhhhhh*. I guess I hear what I can only describe as a sound of nourishment, followed shortly after that by a jarring buzzing one. Off in the distance, I hear, "Fuck, that hurts."

A few feet away, I see a green door with "CIC" in white raised lettering displayed against a black nameplate. Hmm, chief . . . interview . . . chairperson, maybe . . . probably not. Anyway, I give the door a small push, but it's locked. Face to face with the door now, I can notice intricate writing that would easily go unnoticed from afar. I focus on the small letters beneath the nameplate, which contain written general instructions for bypassing the lock. Out-maneuvering this door might be a test. With the directions, it if I, you, US can copy right off I cease to be stopped by this door, is my hunch. Looking around, I realize I'm now standing on a large white mat labeled "EXIT" in big red letters; I'm certain it wasn't there when I approached the door. Well, I did something right . . . I see a door handle, so I grabb it. This time, with no resistance, I push open the door to reveal "101" inscribed in place of "CIC" on the nameplate now. Is this a good sign?

Closing the door behind me, I'm in an even larger room now. Since I'm not back at the entrance, I suppose this must be the right place. The black with gold trim has been replaced with gray—lots of gray, a dull gray—filled with brick and steel, all the same monotonous hue. Nevertheless, to spruce it up, I guess there is some vegetation and signs of life scattered around, though I can't help but notice some pretty fiery-looking plants in the corner. They don't have teeth, do they? Into that plant, I won't peer aroun' an' have a look. I steer clear of those. I navigate through a maze of corridors, moving up and down as I delve deeper into the building. At one point, I pass a large aquarium teeming with jumping fish and little, tiny squids. But one last person stands in my way . . . the receptionist.

She's a real battle-axe of a woman. Twice my size and always angry, she's a hunchbacked beast clad in green to match her piercing eyes. Spiked chokers adorn her wrists and upper arms just above the elbow, rather than her neck like how any sensible woman would wear a choker. It's possible they would have fit the neck of a normal woman, but for her, they seem to fit too tightly, emphasizing her immense stature.

Her mouth, gaping and slack-jawed, is filled with large, gnarly teeth spaced way too far apart. Jump, man, I tell myself—she's breathing fire. I can't comprehend why she's smiling at me. Perhaps it's more of a knowing, ominous grin, aware of what she has waiting for me. I can feel it in my bones; she wants to drop the hammer on me really quick, and sure enough, she lets go of a barrage of them. Quick hands—I didn't even see her make a throwing motion. Fortunately, they go right over my head. I push closer. (Note to self: when issuing HR forms, toss them directly *at* your future employee, not on a looping trajectory). I approach her with caution, knowing that if I get hit, it will knock me down a size, but I won't be dead. She jumps out of her chair—I didn't think someone that size could jump that high—but it gives me an opening. At that point, I also notice she is barefoot—her toenails matching the intensity of her teeth. Just like that, I slip right past her. She makes a one-eighty, still grinning at me, hands clasped, studded chokers on full display, but she knows the end is near. The snarling beast drops out of sight. And, at last, in front of me, a world anew.

"Miyam!" she enthusiastically shouts. Her black pupils locking onto my eyes. Her raised voice startles me, but I'll live. Oy, you'll stop staring at me at some point, right? I think to myself as I approach her. It's evident she has irises, but those must also be dark, blending with her deep, dark pupils to create an indistinguishable boundary between the two. I suppose I could have looked longer, trying to discern that separation, but maintaining eye contact with a young woman of her beauty is nearly impossible for me. I'm sure there are whites to her eyes, but her intense gaze makes me too nervous to find out.

She wears a long, flowing white dress adorned with red trim, cinched tightly around her chest and torso. The fabric fans out from her waist, nearly touching the floor or perhaps even brushing against it. Regardless, it obscured her shoes, leaving me to wonder if she, like the receptionist, is barefoot (is that office policy here?). Her attire, meticulously put together, has everything buttoned up neatly. The red trim of her dress perfectly matches crimson lipstick, which in turn compliments her fiery red locks. Locks—long, flowing locks—reach down to her waist. She exudes an air of royalty . . . not that of a queen, but more akin to her young, elegant daughter; I can almost envision a tiara gracing her beautiful curls.

"I like your jeans," she says. "Jeans are acceptable in this workplace, but genies are not. You'll find out why."

"Oh, umm, OK" I stammered, having no clue what that gal who belongs not working a desk job is saying to me about genies. "Uh, please, call me Ario." My voice cracked ever so slightly on 'Ario.' My palms are sweaty (but for different reasons). She reminds me of a girl, Pauline, whom I once had a crush on, but not anymore.

"Sure," she says cheerily, still holding her polite smile. "So, you don't care for your first name, either?"

"Huh, uh, what?" I stammered again, choking on my words, distracted by how I always hated my father, Otto, for giving me his first name as my middle. (Ugh, why did she have to be so stunning?) "No, not really," I said sheepishly, looking to the floor and breaking eye contact with her. Her dark eyes had drawn me in for too long, and I just had to break away, scratching the back of my neck in the process—a reflex of mine when I'm nervous.

"It's OK, I'll let you in on a little secret," she said, still smiling as she lowered her voice (the volume—not trying to imitate Barry White). "My name's really Filipinas, but everyone calls me 'Peachy.' Her voice raised, and then some. "It fits my outlook on life," she added, her smile growing even larger. "I put in to get a name tag change, ya know, corporate can be kinda slow, but our standard tags will have to do for now. It's like a little quest I'm on to get that name tag changed. All requests must go in this box here." She gestured toward a gray box, roughly the size of a VCR, which also bore a striking resemblance to one. It featured a flip-up top, much like a VCR, where you could place your suggestion inside. "And if that doesn't work for you, send a memo to corporate via fax, and, uh, do what you want. Us lower employees have a little mantra here, which we shortened to 'fax-and-a-do.' But once I didn't have to do it myself, I sent in a fax, and the drinking fountain got fixed."

I glance at her chest, gulping down some extra saliva that accumulated in the back of my throat. That's just what I needed, her suggesting for me to look at her chest. Quickly, I read her name tag, glancing at her to acknowledge that I read it, then back to the floor went my eyeline. 'F.PEREZ.'

"See, wouldn't 'Peachy' make for such a better name tag, more inviting, don't you think? Heck, I'd even settle for

'Peach,' but you could keep yours the same, 'M dot Ario,' I dunno, I like it!" Her voice rose an octave or two on 'like it.' Geez, does she ever break eye contact? It's almost like *she's* enamored with *me*.

She continues, "I guess I should tell you that everyone outside of the office calls me something else, but in here, I keep that 'totes to -uh- like myself.' Oddly, she spoke with a heavy valley girl accent at the end, adding an unexplained and unexpected flair to her speech.

"I mean, you haven't even interviewed here yet, and look at what we're discussing? But you've come this far, so it's not like we're going to send you elsewhere." I couldn't fathom why I would be sent elsewhere; I was certain I was in the right spot. Why would she send me to another level of the building or an entirely different building altogether? Perhaps her instructions made sense, but my nerves clouded my judgment, and I brushed it aside. With Peachy still beaming, I shuffled past her towards the conference room doors, pondering If our paths would ever cross again.

This is it. The moment I've been waiting for. My journey to this pivotal point was met with challenges, but an impossible TASk, it was not. If I have to make this commute again, I think I can do it more quickly. But first, I've got to land this plane. Stepping across the threshold of the interview room, a swell of anticipation courses through me because beyond these doors lies the potential for a future filled with remarkable creativity and profound change. I am / we are teetering on a precipice where success promises an exciting and beautiful new frontier. Still, at the same time, failure means that a once small yet promising evolution will remain grounded, its potential forever constrained by unfulfilled dreams and ideas.

"Ario, please meet Mr. Gunpei and Mr. Shigeru." She directs me with a wave of an open palm to an empty seat in front of a desk where two men are seated. Two men in black suits with colorful ties, both sporting jet-black hair—one with short hair, showing some signs of graying around the temples and sides, while the other has longer hair with a not-so-defined part down the middle stare blankly at me. Both appear very business-like in their mannerisms and attire.

"So," one of them speaks, though I'm unsure which one (the one on the left), "this is a dying industry . . ."

"Maybe already dead," the other chimes in, glancing up from his desk to make eye contact with me on the word 'dead.' One eyebrow inquisitively raised higher than the other.

". . . and *you* want to design video games?" The man on the left ends his inquisition.

"Yeah . . . I have some ideas."

End screen. Power off. Present day.

Easter Eggs Explained

Are you sure you want to play the game using the strategy guide?

"Power On [chapter title] Ready (Player One;)). Start," suggests to the reader that s/he is playing a video game (power the system on and press start on the controller), and "Ready (Player One;))" is a wink and a nod to Ernest Cline's fantastic 2011 book of the same title (sans parentheses and emoticon), which gave me the idea to write a book filled with a bunch of Easter eggs.

"Follow the frog down the hole . . ." refers to the intro of *Blaster Master*, where the protagonist, Jason, follows his pet frog, Fred—who has just come in contact with a radioactive box—down a hole. In the realm of NES video games, it's a great McGuffin and the most memorable to the author.

"I'm third-generation here," refers to the NES being a third-generation home video console.

". . . [I]n a place called Redmond," refers to Redmond, Washington, which is the location of the Nintendo of America headquarters.

"We're approaching Easter. Eggs . . . " is a not-so-veiled reference to Easter eggs.

"I loved finding them, but now that I'm older, I take a lot more joy in hiding them," refers to me hiding Easter eggs in the book.

"If you saw me, I'd look like I'm in my early twenties, but I could be any age . . ." refers to a video game character's sprite looking a specific way, but a person of any age can play the game.

"Palms are sweaty," refers to my frequently sweating hands when playing video games (my hands are actually getting a little clammy while typing this line, similar to how I start to salivate a little when I think about hot sauce). I purposely didn't write *my* palms are sweaty, because the sweaty palms are not of the narrator/character, Ario, but instead of you, the player of the video game. Since "Palms are sweaty," is referenced often, I wanted to introduce it early by having Ario mention, "Palms are sweaty." There are only three uses of "My palms are sweaty" in the book: in the *Metal Gear* level when Solid Snake is trapped in the room; in the *Punch-Out!!* level, which refers to Little Mac's palms being sweaty because his hands are wrapped and stuffed in boxing gloves; and, in the Final Level when Ario talks to Peach.

". . . Koji left it here some time ago before his parents divorced, and he moved into that condo with his mom and her new boyfriend," refers to Koji Kondo, the music composer behind so many NES games, notably *Super Mario Bros.* and *The Legend of Zelda*.[3]

"Du, du, du, dah-da, du, doop, the melody goes . . ." is the opening few notes to the *Super Mario Bros.* theme.

"It plays in my head, bouncing in and out, fading away and returning again," refers to a game's music

[3] Wikipedia contributors. (2024, January 25). Koji Kondo. In Wikipedia. Retrieved January 25, 2024 https://en.wikipedia.org/wiki/Koji_Kondo

always being there, but the player noticing it and not noticing it at other times.

". . . [S]ometimes the tempo picks up when it gets near the end of the song . . ." refers to the *Super Mario Bros.* in-world music which gets faster when the timer reaches ninety-nine.

"(Louis is my closest friend; he's like a brother to me. We actually look quite similar, though he's a bit taller and leaner, and most of the time, he can jump higher than me)," refers to the characters Mario and Luigi's resemblance, but Luigi is taller and thinner. Luigi often has a higher jumping ability than Mario in most games (but the higher jumping ability can come at the expense of traction).

"Eventually, his moniker got the first letter of his surname attached to it. Not by me. We don't know how or by whom. But I liked the sound of it, so I ran with it. Try saying it out loud," refers to Luigi (obviously).

"Maybe I fell into another pit," refers to how easy it is for the E.T. character to fall into a pit.

". . . [I]t's like *E.T.* killed the buzz around video games," refers to *E.T.* being thought of as the sole reason the video game industry crashed in 1983, but it was only a contributing factor.

"What a shock to the system the whole thing was," refers to the 1983 crash of the video game industry being known in Japan as Atari Shock.[4]

"*E.T.* had potential, but it felt so rushed to me," refers to Atari's need to rush development of the *E.T.* game to get it out before Christmas. Atari gave game designer Howard Scott Warsaw just five weeks to develop the game.[5]

---

[4] Wikipedia contributors. (2024, February 20). Video game crash of 1983. In Wikipeddia. Retrieved February 20, 2024, from https://en.wikipedia.org/wiki/Video_game_crash_of_1983

[5] Wikipedia contributors. (2024, February 15). E.T. the Extra-Terrestrial (video game). In Wikipedia. Retrieved February 15, 2024, https://en.wikipedia.org/wiki/E.T._the_Extra-Terrestrial_(video_game)

"With this game in particular, it felt like the developers just phoned it in and went home . . . or maybe they went home first and then phoned it in," refers to the commonly misquoted *E.T.* line (when said in E.T.'s voice), "E.T. phone home." But the correct quote is, "E.T. home phone." The kids, Gertie and Elliot, say, "E.T. phone home."

"A fellow gamer nerd, Jimmy Hecker . . ." is an alias for James Heller, the former Atari manager who was in charge of the *E.T.* burial; he admitted to the *Associated Press* that 728,000 cartridges of various games (not just *E.T.*) were buried in an Alamogordo, New Mexico landfill;[6] the 2014 documentary *Atari: Game Over* enjoyably tells this story well.

"*If I ever have a daughter, I think I would name her after his wife* is the last thought in my head before I drift off to sleep," refers to *The Legend of Zelda* series creator Shigeru Miyamoto naming the game after F. Scott's Fitzgerald's wife, Zelda; and refers to Robin Williams naming his daughter, Zelda, too.[7]

"Our neighbor has a spare key, Saul. Oh, man . . ." refers to *Solomon's Key*.

"I pause for a second to take a beat and to collect my thoughts," refers to utilizing the pause feature of many games when the action gets tough and you need a little [bathroom] break.

". . . [O]nly a handful of playing cards in its place. Retrieving them: a jack, queen, king, joker, and ace . . ." refers to the different keys in *Faxanadu*: the Jack Key, the Queen Key, and so on.

---

[6] Wikipedia contributors. (2024, February 15). E.T. the Extra-Terrestrial (video game). In Wikipedia. Retrieved February 15, 2024, https://en.wikipedia.org/wiki/E.T._the_Extra-Terrestrial_(video_game)

[7] Jenkins, D. (n.d.). The Legend of Zelda Name Origin Explained. TheGamer. Retrieved February 9, 2024, from https://www.thegamer.com/the-legend-of-zelda-name-origin-explained/#:~:text=In%20an%20interview%20with%20Amazon,the%20very%20first%20Zelda%20title.%22

"I turn the deadbolt knob to unlock the door as I step into the darkness," is a callback to when Ario initially encountered the garage service door, and he needed a key to unlock it. However, upon his return, the presence of the deadbolt knob signified a change. Armed with the keys, the door was now passable, akin to unlocking a door (or the next level) in a video game. Additionally, "into the darkness" reminds me of some of *The Legend of Zelda*'s transition screens between rooms where the screen would go from light to dark (like when entering an unlit room) or from light to dark to light (like when entering an underground item room in a dungeon).

Level 1: Rad Racer & Paperboy

". . . [I]s my 328 Twin Turbo," refers to one of the two car choices in *Rad Racer*.

"I give a quick rub to my little F1 Machine toy car dangling from the rear-view mirror . . ." refers to the option of selecting the F1 Machine instead of the 328 Twin Turbo.

"The freshly waxed red paint job pairs beautifully with black leather seat faces and two-toned gray dashboard, door panels, and interior," refers to the car's colors being used to describe an NES controller.

"The . . . steering wheel I installed is shaped like the letter D, with the letter's hump pointing up. I look left, then right . . . then down at the dash," refers to the controller's so-called D-pad; "up," "left," "right," and "down" are the directionals used for movement on the D-pad.

"The two big red circles on the dash always stand out to me: two -ometers, speed- on the left and a tach- on the right," refers to the left [B button] on the NES controller because it was used to run [speed] in *Super Mario Bros.*, but it was also used to attack, however, I chose to specifically use "a tach" instead of just "tach" to have you mimic the sound of "attack."

"I'm wired and ready to go," refers to the wire connecting the controller to the NES game system.

"My garage is painted sky blue to match my house, and the whole thing's topped with a gray roof. My neighbors to the left and right of me have brick houses with black roofs," refers to the houses on the *Paperboy* map. Depicted on the screen before gameplay begins, there are only two colors of houses shown: blue houses, which are paperboy's customers, and red houses, which are not paperboy's customers.

"I nearly hit a kid on his bike," refers to the playable *Paperboy* character.

". . . [H]auling ass on his bike, slinging *The Daily Sun* . . ." refers to the newspaper the paperboy delivers.

"Maybe he's so good because there's a training course at the end of my street," refers to the training course that concludes each level of *Paperboy*.

"Oh, and I don't know the story, but I guess he once stopped a thief, too. What a true hero," refers to the front page of *The Daily Sun*, that mentions the paperboy stopping a thief and the paper calls him a hero.

"I live on a vibrant street. I walk down it, and I have dodge radio-controlled cars, that punk skateboard kid, and another asshole breakdancing on the sidewalk," refers to obstacles in *Paperboy*.

"I recall one time strolling down the street and a goddamn tire took my ass out. Did I trip over it? No, that fucker was rolling down a driveway and took out my legs. And that was shortly after I dodged a lawn jockey running across my path," refers to more in-game obstacles.

"Is the village ever going to get that section of sidewalk fixed?" refers to the obstacle of the construction worker jack-hammering the sidewalk.

"And why do some of my neighbors have headstones in their front yards?" refers to in-game imagery.

"I saw the Grim Reaper once—it must've been Halloween, but that doesn't feel right," refers to an in-game obstacle.

"It doesn't make sense to me that I get my paper delivered, but a stack of tied-up newspapers is also sitting on my driveway," refers to some customers getting their paper delivered, but also having a stack of newspapers on their driveway. The stack of newspapers reloads the paperboy's newspaper count.

"Get this: when the paperboy finishes his route, he comes across random dudes sitting in the park cheering him on," refers to the conclusion of the *Paperboy* training course where random men are sitting in the stands.

"I start on Sunset Boulevard with one goal in mind. To keep me on track, I have checkpoints in my head that I must reach by a specific time," refers to the *Rad Racer* map showing "Course 1 Sunset Coastline" with a start and a goal, plus dots for course checkmarks.

". . . [K]icking up a cloud of dust in my wake," refers to the graphic in *Rad Racer* when the player hits the accelerator button.

"I push the RPMs to the max, redlining at 158 mph," refers to the maximum speed in *Rad Racer* of 255 KMH, which is 158 MPH.

"A flash of olive drab from an out-of-control military jeep careens into my lane, cutting me off. I began shouting, 'Hey, you jacka—' luckily . . ." refers to the military jeep in *Jackal*.

"POW!" [the word choice is for the sound of two cars crashing into each other] refers to the objective of *Jackal*, which is to rescue POWs (Prisoners of War).

"Squinting into my side view mirror, I see what remains of it—not much. Err! What a 'deyyyck' that driver was!" refers to two members of the Jackal unit: Sergeant

Quint, and, the leader of the Jackal unit, Colonel Decker.

". . . [M]akes your blood boil when people drive like that. Good luck . . ." refers to introductory screen quote for *Jackal*, which reads, "This battle will make your blood boil. Good luck!"

". . . [A]s I make it to Grand Canyon Avenue passing my favorite grease joint, 'Ruins of Athens Gyros,' along the way," refers to the names of two in-game courses.

"I flip through the channels, but only three come in," refers to being able to cycle through three types of songs in the game by pressing the 'select' button on the controller.

"It's like the drivers are trying to force me off the road," refers to a point in the game when cars are actively trying to hit the player's car.

"That sends the 328 airborne. Flipping over, I land on the roof with enough force to bounce me back upright," refers to what happens when the car crashes in *Rad Racer*.

"The last thing I recall is hearing DJ Jenny on Resistance Radio, 120.48 on the dial," refers to the radio waveband frequency used to contact resistance member, Jennifer, in *Metal Gear*.

"She can be a bit of a snob, but I like her. If we ever meet, she would see I'm pretty classy," refers to the hostage in *Metal Gear* that gives Solid Snake Jennifer's radio frequency. The hostage also warns Solid Snake, "She can be a snob, but she probably won't answer unless you are pretty classy."

Level 2: Metal Gear

"Is this heaven? Am I having an out[er] of body experience?" refers to the Outer Heaven Resistance movement in *Metal Gear,* called Outer Heaven that occupied the base called Outer Heaven in South Africa.

". . . [M]y chute is gone, too; in its place is a pack of smokes," refers to Solid Snake's only item in the equipment screen to start the game being a pack of cigarettes.

"Man, I'm rank," refers to Solid Snake's "RANK" shown on the game screen. It starts at one star and can go as high as four stars. Having a higher rank allows Solid Snake a higher health meter and to carry more ammunition and rations.

"I see some stars in the sky, and one big star stands out," refers to the one-star rank when Solid Snake starts the game.

"Goddamn, what's this buzzing in my ear? That's not a bug . . ." refers to the transceiver sound when Solid Snake gets a call (later called 'CODEC' beginning in *Metal Gear Solid* for PlayStation, it's titled 'TRANSCEIVER' in *Metal Gear*).

"Jeff Grande with an 'e,' but the 'e' is silent," refers to "jefe grande," which is Spanish for "big boss."

"I'm trying to get a boss," refers to getting (killing) Big Boss, who appears to be the player's aid in the game but, ultimately, proves to be the enemy.

"A 'grey' fox scurries across my path—it looks lost," refers to the in-game quote displayed when Solid Snake first accesses the transceiver, "First, attempt to contact missing our 'grey fox.'"

"I'm getting sleepy; I feel asleep," refers to the grammatically incorrect quote from an NPC in *Metal Gear*. Grammatically incorrect text was somewhat commonplace in the translation of Japanese games to the American market. "Uh-oh, the truck have started to move," refers to the on-screen text when the player enters the truck near the closed gate, which is another example of grammatically incorrect text.

"I find a gas mask, and I hear Jeff Grande in my ear. He tells me to use the gas mask in gas-filled areas," refers to Big Boss telling Solid Snake to use the gas mask in gas-filled areas.

"He warns me, 'not to let enemy detect you,'" refers to text from Big Boss displayed on the screen which omits the definite article 'the.'

"Did Schneider fart in here?" refers to releasing the hostage, Schneider, and then proceeding into the next room, which is gas-filled.

". . . [D]odging a giant ass rolling pin along the way," refers to the many item rooms that have a giant rolling pin cascading across the floor.

"Let me just scan my key card to get through this door. Nope. How about this one? OK. Let's try this one. Alright, the fourth time's a charm," refers to not knowing which key card opens a door, so the player must cycle through them until finding the right one. For example, a door that can be opened with key card one cannot be opened with a "higher level" card key, like two, for example. This was changed in later *Metal Gear* games.

"I'm told to talk to Diane because she can help me, but, of course, she's out shopping," refers to a freed hostage telling Solid Snake to reach Diane on waveband 120.33. When Solid Snake does, he's greeted by Steve because Diane is out shopping.

"I find out the cardboard box comes in handy a time or two," refers to using the cardboard box to move undetected by cameras.

"And guess what: when I find some ammo, all I have to do is call Jeff on the transceiver, and when I end the call, there's more ammo again, right in the same spot. It works for food, too," refers to the transceiver hack of being able to max out on ammo, missiles, mines, and rations.

"Man, I'm even more rank now than before," refers to Solid Snake's increasing rank throughout the game.

"Shit! I'm captured. 'Under arrest!?!'" refers to entering a truck that leads to Solid Snake's capture and the guard telling Solid Snake he's under arrest. It advances the story line because it puts Solid Snake into a cell next to the secret location where Grey Fox is being held hostage. Solid Snake needs to punch the wall to enter the Grey Fox's holding cell.

". . . I have to see Dr. Pettrovich (the real one) and have it checked out," refers to Grey Fox explaining to Solid Snake that Dr. Pettrovich, who invented Metal Gear, is the only one who can destroy it; (the real one) refers to the fake Dr. Pettrovich found in the game.

"Hopefully, his receptionist, Ellen, will be in the office that day; she's cute . . . and I think she's into some kinky stuff,too," refers to Dr. Pettrovich's daughter, Ellen, who is tied up when Solid Snake finds her.

"I wonder if Jeff is giving it to me straight or if this is all just a big boss lie . . ." refers to Big Boss telling Solid Snake to retreat ("Operation 'Intrude N313' canceled. Repeat, canceled. Return to base immediately! This is an order!") at a point in the game, and to being 'advised' to get into the truck—the truck that takes Solid Snake back to the area near the beginning of the game. At the final boss battle, Big Boss tells Solid Snake, ". . . as a new and inexperienced member of our team, you were supposed to be tricked into carrying false information."

". . . I duck, but I'm no coward," refers to the Coward Duck enemy Solid Snake fights near the end of the game. "That was a close call," refers to the released hostages always telling Solid Snake, "That was a close call," upon their rescue.

"It's all over, at last," refers to Solid Snake at the conclusion of the game reporting back to the Big Boss (after building two) on radio waveband 120.13: "It's all over - - - everything, at last! Solid Snake returning to base. Over."

"One final buzz in my ear, a new waveband: 120.77. Time to meet my creator(s)," refers to the ending screen where Solid Snake can move the transceiver waveband to 120.77 and get the game's final message: "This is station KNK bringing you a spot news report. Today at dawn there was apparently a large scale earth tremor in the region of Galzburg, South Africa - - - this is your computer speaking. Here are the creators of your metal gear game."

Level 3: Mike Tyson's Punch-Out!!

"Ding, ding, ding," refers to the sound of the fight bell that signals the opening of *Mike Tyson's Punch-Out!!*.

". . . [G]reen in color—oddly, they're only green when I box, white when I'm at rest—matching my shorts," refers to Little Mac's gloves and shorts changing from white to green when he walks to the center of the boxing ring.

"Yeah, yeah . . . I'm Doc," refers to Little Mac's trainer's name, which is Doc Louis.

". . . [H]is fist pumping without stopping," refers to Doc Louis' never-ending fist pumping mechanic during the in between rounds trainer talk.

"Stick and move, stick and move!" refers to one of Doc Louis' pre-round advice quotes.

"I'm your trainer, but don't get any ideas like those other guys cornering—freaking weird! Sure, they got better boxing techniques, but there are just some things as a trainer I WON'T do . . . well, not anymore, at least!" refers to *Ring King*. As a boxing game, it was overshadowed by *Punch-Out!!*

but it featured a far more accurate boxing simulation. The game allowed players to move about the ring, throw various punches, and even grapple (which looked like two men slow dancing in a loving embrace). The in between rounds trainer "talk" literally looked like the trainer was fellating the boxer (seriously, look it up), and that's why Doc says, ". . . [T]here are just some things as a trainer I WON'T do."

"I need to plan something fast, a little machination if you will," refers to the boxer's name, Little Mac.

"'Round, 'round, 'round, I go," refers to the three rounds for each fight.

"I have a lot of heart, I tell you; maybe I can be a star, but I'm a zero right now," refers to Little Mac having a heart counter for stamina and a star counter for power punches. In his first fight, which is against Glass Joe, Little Mac starts with nineteen hearts but zero stars.

"This joeker across from me with the glassy look in his eyes . . ." refers to Glass Joe.

"I pop him with a couple of right hooks, and he's seeing stars now," refers to specific punches from Little Mac that generate stars for power punches. When one is earned, a star flashes above the opponent's head.

". . . I'm going to dance like a fly and bite like a mosquito . . ." refers to one of Doc Louis' lines, "Dancin' like a fly, bite like a mosquito."

"Let me start you off with one of these," refers to the player pressing the 'start' button on the controller to deliver a power punch.

"What's with the 'hey you' eyebrows sent my direction?" refers to Piston Honda's very animated eyebrows.

"This guy's relentless; he's got a motor on him like a Honda," refers to Piston Honda.

"It's over, ladies and gentlemen!" refers to after the minor circuit title fight screen where Little Mac is shown, and the on-screen display reads, "Ladies and Gentlemen!"

"We have a new champion!!"

"Ahh, it's time to relax in my pink jumpsuit . . ." refers to Little Mac's pink jumpsuit he wears during the jogging training scenes.

"Well, you can't just stand there like a statue, lady, you can't take liberties with this game," refers to the post-title fight training scenes where Little Mac runs behind Doc Louis, who is on a bike, ending at the Statue of Liberty, also known as Lady Liberty.

"If you can do this, maybe I'll give you a pass." "Word," I reply refers to the password the player receives at the end of the training session.

"WOMEN . . . WEAKEN . . . LEGS!!!" refers not to an NES game but to the classic line from Rocky's trainer, Mickey (played by Burgess Meredith), in *Rocky* (one of my favorite movies and one of my favorite lines).

"There's a minor problem here that's about to become something more significant. I got more boxing to do, sir. Cut to the next fight . . ." refers to Little Mac being the champ of the Minor Circuit, but now he'll face tougher opponents in the Major Circuit.

"Look at this guy entering the ring with a flower in his mouth," refers to Don Flamenco's ring entrance.

"I dance all over him . . ." refers to the Spanish flamenco dance that Don Flamenco is clearly named after.

". . . [H]it him with alternating left and right shots to the grill. I make easy work of him," refers to how the player can knock down Don Flamenco with alternating jabs to his face, not getting stopped until Flamenco is knocked down.

"Open up, fat boy! I got a knuckle sandwich for you. X marks the spot. I pop this guy so hard I knock his pants off. Enough shots to the belly, and he drops. He's unable to get up. You've got to be joking; maybe he broke his hipp, oh, that would be a bad way to go out," refers to King Hippo, his appearance, how to defeat him, and how the fight progresses.

"Oh, great. This guy's wearing a skinned tiger for a robe," refers to Great Tiger and the skinned tiger robe that rests on the belt buckle in his corner, which is seen in between rounds.

"This guy was like a great magician out there; I was charmed by his punches," refers to Doc advising Mac about Great Tiger: "His father was a great magician in India. Don't be charmed by his magic punches."

"It's been no fun club today, that's for sure," refers to Doc telling Mac, "Join the Nintendo Fun Club today! Mac." This is the response to Little Mac saying, "Help! Doc!!"

"Who's the giant bald man charging at me!?!" refers to the Bull Charge from Bald Bull.

"What was once a constant and noble approach to this game has turned my adversary into an instant bull in the ring," refers to how Istanbul (where Bald Bull is from) was once known as Constantinople AND instant "bull" also ties into the opponent's name. Two Easter eggs for the price of one, baby!

"I'm a major boxer now, sir, cuz . . ." refers to the title fight versus Bald Bull. It is for the W.V.B.A Major Circuit.

". . . I'm going to stand up to him, face his charge, and watch . . ." refers to Doc Louis' advice, "Mac! Watch his Bull Charge! Stand up to him!"

"My shots are getting stronger, to the point where every punch I land to my opponent's face sends his eyes spinning like the reel of a slot machine," refers to most boxers from Bald Bull and after whose eyes roll back and flash when punched in the face.

". . . [I]t's time to cool down with a soda pop," refers to Little Mac's next never-before-seen opponent, Soda Popinski (he has a rematch with Piston Honda after the Bald Bull fight).

"*HAH-HAH-HAH*," refers to Soda Popinski's laugh.

"I'm getting tired; I turn pink with lethargy . . ." refers to Little Mac's heart gauge hitting zero and tiring him out, he turns pink and is unable to punch—only dodge—until his stamina comes back.

". . . [P]inko stinko opponent," refers to the shade of pink that is Soda Popinski, but it also refers to the slanderous term for a lighter form of communist (pink being a lighter form of red) because Popisnki is from Moscow, U.S.S.R.

"Maybe I need some steak or a lovely Spanish rosé to boost my energy," refers to rematches between Bald Bull and Don Flamenco (who is from Madrid, Spain; Don Flamenco still has a rose in his mouth pre-fight).

"What should I select? Doc's never-ending pumping fist pumps faster now," refers to the player's ability in between rounds to hit the 'select' button on the controller to get a health meter boost; Doc will pump his fist faster when it's been activated. A player can do this cheat before the first round (Doc will again pump his fist faster), but Mac's health gauge—which is full to start the round—will decrease by half. Additionally, this health cheat can only be done once per fight.

"I feel rejuvenated, but the guy across from me wants to put me to sleep," refers to Mr. Sandman.

"My star is brighter now . . ." refers to being able to accumulate more stars in later fights because the fights go longer.

"Did you know the first 800 phone number was 800-422-2602? But if you called it, it was always a busy signal," refers to the *Punch-Out!!* code, when called on a phone, yielded a busy signal. The number was for Nintendo of America's old customer service line.[8]

". . . I need to dodge his punch and then counter-punch," refers to direct advice from Doc.

"Oh, super, another macho man of a fighter. He's got a real Hollywood look to him," refers to Little Mac's pen-

---

[8] IGN. (n.d.). NES Cheats - Mike Tyson's Punch-Out!! - Mike Tyson's Punch-Out!! Wiki Guide - IGN. Retrieved February 9, 2024, from https://www.ign.com/wikis/mike-tysons-punch-out/NES_Cheats

ultimate opponent, Super Macho Man, who is from Hollywood, California.

"He can flex his pecs . . ." refers to Super Macho Man taunt of Little Mac before the round begins and after he knocks down Little Mac

". . . [B]ut he's dizzied now," refers to Super Macho Man's two styles of spinning punches.

"With no help from the cameraman, the bearded man, or the bespectacled man, I'm on my own," refers to certain people in the crowd helping the player's punch timing during fights with Piston Honda, Bald Bull, and Super Macho Man.

"This is a story of true victory," refers to the greeting the player receives during the introduction after meeting Little Mac and Doc Louis.

"In a flash . . ." refers to Mike Tyson flashing before throwing a punch.

". . . [L]ike a stick of dynamite went off, kid," refers to Mike Tyson's nickname, "Kid Dynamite."

"Is that a Bronx cheer?" refers to Little Mac being from the Bronx, New York.

". . . I guess my fingers just weren't fast enough," refers to the onscreen message from Mike Tyson after beating him, "Great fighting!! You were tough, Mac! I've never seen such finger speed before."

"'Mister, are you a dream?'" refers to the license to use the Tyson name and the likelihood of it expiring, thus the Tyson character was replaced by the fictional, Mr. Dream.

"'I tried to keep it clean,'" refers to the message at the start of the game: "Let's keep it clean! Now come out boxing!" which the player receives after hitting 'start' at the title screen when the boxing glove punches through the image.

Level 4: Tecmo Bowl

"We must have had their same play called, a run to the left off tackle . . ." refers to choosing the same play the offense chose, thus being able to stop their play. A run to the left off tackle is one of two LA Raiders' run plays; the other being a sweep to the right.

"Even though the game has already started, it's another coin flip," refers to most *Tecmo Bowl* teams having two run plays and two pass plays. Therefore, if it seems like an obvious passing down, it's a fifty / fifty coin flip if the player will correctly guess the opposition's play.

"It's a run; we guessed that right, but, boy, we don't know everything," refers to the Bo Knows ad campaign.

"It's like they didn't even try to block him, or maybe they couldn't stop him," refers to Lawrence Taylor's ability to get through any special teams' offensive line virtually unblocked.

Level 5: Metroid

"The room is spinning. Wait . . . I'm spinning," refers to Samus' ability to curl up into a ball after obtaining the Maru Mari, which is available shortly after starting the game.

"Uniquely, the suit has a very curvy design, almost effeminate in its appearance," refers to the clever end-game twist that the suit covers a female character, making it one of the best end-game surprises of all NES games.

"As I zoom through it, I just start blasting; some enemies are killed while others are unaffected . . . what a ripp-off," refers to spikey creatures that move around ledges who are called Zoomers and to the so-called Ripper creature that can't be killed with Samus' regular beam.

"Maybe in a different world, I could enter these pipes . . . what a warped thought," refers to *Super Mario Bros.* and being able to enter the sewer pipes; and how some pipes are used for warp points to other worlds.

". . . I notice the unclaimed energy bump hovering above the sewer blocks other baddies from coming out after me. Hmm, I can use this to my advantage," refers to intentionally avoiding picking up an energy bump or missile above a sewer because it blocks other enemies from emerging, thereby giving the player a temporary break from the barrage of enemies.

". . . [S]o I select to give these missiles a try," refers to the player pressing the 'select' button on the controller to switch from blaster to missiles.

"It's a long shot, but it works!" refers to the long beam power-up Samus obtains early in the game.

"High-five! But nobody other than this statue is around to give me one . . ." refers to the five missiles needed to open a red door and how the Chozo statue sits with its hands open and flat offering Samus a power-up.

". . . [A]nd his hands are affixed low . . . err, low-five it is, is what I chose. Oh . . ." refers to the Chozo humanoid alien species that possess bird-like traits and characteristics.

". . . I'm just going to curl up in a ball, perch myself on this statue's open palms, and take a little respite, too, where no one can see me," refers to Samus doing this game-play mechanic and then being able not to be seen on the screen once the power-up cloak respawns.

"It worked—nnnnn-ice!" refers to bombing the floor and then falling through the yellow pit to make one's way to the ice beam.

"Then it dawns on me: when faced with a barrier, I cannot waver in my determination, and I need to take a variance to my approach to traversing this planet. Soon, I'll learn it's a method that suits me well," refers to the path of going through the ceiling and then using a frozen waver as a jumping-off point to ultimately get the varia suit. The varia suit's name comes from the Japanese to English mistranslation of the word "barrier." The suit usually provides extra defense and allows Samus to explore high(er) temperature areas, so the suit is more of a barrier against harsher environments and attacks.[9]

"Fucking shit! I'm stuck in the ceiling!" refers to the Samus sprite getting stuck in the respawned blocks.

"Goddammit! I went through a door, and some fucker followed me to the next room, hitting me in the process when I transitioned between rooms and was unable to defend myself," refers to this event happening quite frequently in *Metroid* when the Samus sprite is essentially locked while going through a door, but the NPC enemies can still move thus causing damage to Samus as she's unable to defend herself.

"Screw 'em, I jump and spin right through them, attacking in the process," refers to the Screw Attack, which is one of the most-bad ass attacks in any NES game.

"Aww, sweet. A random energy tank is lying on the floor. I don't have to work for this one; it *could* be too good to be true, but fuck it, I'm so excited, I'll just run full speed after it," refers to the seemingly easy-to-grab energy tank in the corridor between doors, but there are two columns of fake floor tiles Samus must jump over to grab the energy tank.

". . . I blast away, never relenting; it of this world, I rid, leaving . . ." refers to the mini-boss, Ridley.

"Thinking back, raiding . . ." refers to the mini-boss, Kraid.

"A jellyfish with giant fangs darts over and latches on the life of ***me t***o ***ro***b; ***I'd*** . . ." refers to a metroid.

"Oh! Is that spaghetti?" refers to the rinka, which are rings of burning energy that look like SpaghettiOs—a staple of a 1980's lunch or dinner.

"Oh, if they were, I would cheer," refers to the rinka also resembling Cheerios, another staple of a 1980's cuisine, but this time for breakfast . . . or lunch . . . . . . or dinner.

---

[9] Hofmann, C. (n.d.). A Look at the Metroid Series: Varia Suit. Legends of Localization. Retrieved February 9, 2024, from https://legendsoflocalization.com/a-look-at-the-metroid-series-varia-suit/

"It's like time is slowing down," refers to the NES game engine being unable to finish the tasks of a single frame within the time it takes for the NES to display a frame. It generally seems to occur when there are a lot of sprites on the screen, but that's not the case according to the forum author, 'tokumaru.'[10]

"There she is . . . the mother of all enemies. I, on this ***mother*** with aplom***b, rain*** . . ." refers to Mother Brain.

". . . [A] time bomb was set. I need to get out fast!" refers to the on-screen message of "time bomb set get out fast!"

". . . [T]his just in, bail? Eyeing a chance to start over pass as words through my mind," refers to the Justin Bailey password that: gives Samus a bunch of powerups, has Ridley and Kraid defeated, and—most famously—has Samus shed her protective suit revealing her sexy leotard-clad body.

---

[10] Forum thread: Rainwarrior. (2016, October 20). Slowdowns and What Causes Them. NESDev Forum. Retrieved February 9,2024,from https://forums.nesdev.org/viewtopic.php?t=11040#:~:text=Slowdowns%20happen%20when%20the%20game,data%20for%20the%20next%20frame.

Level 6: Mega Man

"Contrary to pictures of me holding a pistol, my suit still features a built-in hand cannon," refers to the NES box cover art for *Mega Man* and *Mega Man 2* depicting Mega Man with two human hands and one hand holding a pistol. The cover art for *Mega Man 3* accurately depicts the suit with the built-in hand cannon that is seen on the sprite in the *Mega Man* games.

"Oddly, every time I jump, I need to open my mouth," refers to the Mega Man sprite opening his mouth agape every time he jumps.

"OHHH, FUCK! My disembodied head is lying on the ground," refers to Mega Man's extra lives / one-ups being his head.

"Toothy-smiled green beanies are swooping in, trying to hit me . . ." refers to the Bunby Heli enemy found in the Guts Man, Cut Man, Wily Stage 2 stages.

"I've got guts, man! Bombs away," refers to using bombs to get past the Guts Man boss.

"I progress through blasting what resembles an erecting metal phallus, shooting white projectiles at me," refers to the wall-mounted gun with a beak-like armored shell that opens and closes. Upon opening and extending, it fires a white pellet at Mega Man. They are found in Cut Man, Bomb Man, and Wily Stage 2 stages.

"A jumping robot hits me, and it hurts—easy there, big guy," refers to Big Eye, which is a large one-eyed jumping robot that tries to crush Mega Man. It does a good amount of attack damage and is found in many stages of the game.

"A couple of block throws cut deep, and my opponent is quickly sliced and diced," refers to using the Guts Man ability of lifting and throwing blocks. Hitting Cut Man with two blocks defeats him.

"There's so much action going on I feel time is slowing down and I'm sluggish," refers to the NES game engine unable to finish the tasks of a single frame within the time it takes for the NES to display a frame. [Refer to footnote 10 for citation.] This was referenced in the *Metroid* level since the slow frame rate would happen frequently in NES games.

"What a charge this stage has been! I bolt up the ladder and gash my next opponent with two well-placed slashes," refers to the Elec Man stage and how climbing the ladder allows Mega Man to enter his lair from below. Two hits with the Cut Man blade ends Elec Man.

"Sliding on ice, I fall into the water, astonishingly, without making a splash," refers to Mega Man (in the ice stage) entering the water without making a splash.

"I find myself in a large, empty room with no way to escape. Fortunately, some random blocks appear; they aid my ascent, but they're extremely tough to cross," refers to much of the Ice Man level utilizing disappearing and reappearing blocks and moveable platforms to get through the level.

"It's been a wily goose chase thus far. Will it continue?" refers to the saying, 'wild goose chase,' but 'wily' refers to Dr. Wily, the main protagonist in *Mega Man*. Additionally, 'goose' and 'Will it continue?' hint (albeit small) at the next level.

"But I have no fire to melt the ice, man," refers to the *Mega Man* boss, Ice Man, and leads into the next level.

Level 7: Top Gun

"These enemies are dangerous and foolish . . . I might be worse, but you want me on your side," refers to the *Top Gun* Iceman quote: "Maverick, it's not your flying, it's your attitude. The enemy's dangerous, but right now you're worse. Dangerous and foolish. You may not like who's flying with you, but whose side are you on?"

"I make quick work of them with my wing-mounted rapid-fire barrel machine guns unleashing great balls of fire," refers to "The Great Balls of Fire" song/scene in *Top Gun*.

"Hounded by enemies, I rip off a few missiles . . ." refers to the T-11 Hound missiles the player can choose before the mission starts.

". . . [Q]uantity over quality," refers to choosing forty T-11 Hound missiles with a power level of one for the first mission.

"A bird joins my starboard side. Hey, tiger. Hell, I'd . . ." refers to the helicopter shooter game, *Tiger-Heli*.

"Midway through my run, a flash of lightning rips through the sky. . . . I heed its warning and lock on to it . . ." refers to *1942*, where the player pilots a World War II-era Lockheed P-38 Lightning combat plane. *1942* is set in the Pacific Theater of World War II and is loosely based on the Battle of Midway; however, *1942* was followed by *1943: The Battle of Midway*.

"Is that a Russian attacking me?" refers to *Rush'n Attack*, the phonetically equivalent title for a game released during the heightened tensions of the Cold War. During this period, both games and movies often featured Russian and communist adversaries as primary antagonists. This trend reflected the pervasive cultural atmosphere, where fears of nuclear conflicts and ideological rivalry between East and West permeated various forms of media.

"That devil barrel rolls out of sight," refers to the German nickname for the P-38, the "fork-tailed devil."[11] The barrel roll in *1942* was a neat in-game maneuver.

"Only an ace can fly like that in that old thing," refers to an American Fighter Ace, a term for a fighter pilot who has destroyed five or more enemy aircraft in aerial combat."In my earpiece, I hear, 'Captain, look over there in the sky, a hawk has joined us,'" refers to *Captain Skyhawk* (one of my favorite games . . . and a game I beat).

"Fuel low! Speed up! Speed up! Speed up! Left! Left! Right! Right! Down! Down! Connected," refers to the on-screen commands for mid-air refueling.

"Technology is amazing: not only can I refuel mid-air, but I can also reload missiles," refers to how mid-air refueling also reloads missiles.

"Danger!" refers to "Danger!" flashing across the radar screen when an enemy plane approaches from behind the player's fighter jet.

---

[11] Lockheed Martin. (n.d.). P-38 Lightning: The Fork-Tailed Devil. Retrieved February 27, 2024, from https://www.lockheedmartin.com/en-us/news/features/history/p-38.html

". . . [L]et's turn and burn," refers to a quote from Nick in *Top Gun*.

"Hard left, hard right, hard left, hard right, I lost him," refers to moving left and right in the game to shake the enemy off your tail.

"I don't have time to think up here; if I think, I'm dead," refers to the Maverick quote, "you don't have time to think up there. If you think, you're dead."

"Hair on fire . . ." refers to Charlie telling Maverick, "You're not going to be happy unless you're going Mach two with your hair on fire."

". . . [F]lying by the seat of my pants, no one can predict my next move," refers to Jester's report on Maverick, "His fitness report says it all. Flies by the seat of his pants, totally unpredictable."

"Don't 'Easy there, tiger,' me; I'm a one-man wolf pack," refers to choosing the twenty T-22 Wolf missiles with a power level of two, which offers a balance of power and quantity after the first mission, rather than choosing the ten T-33 Tiger missiles with a power level of four. The double power level of the Tiger missiles is not worth having half the quantity of the Wolf missiles.

"It's been a wild goose chase up here . . ." refers to Maverick's wingman, Goose.

". . . [N]ot a walk in the park . . ." refers to a Maverick line said to Iceman: "Just a walk in the park, Kazansky."

". . . [F]or this free spirit," refers to maverick, a synonym for free spirit.

"I could tell you more, but it's classified, and then I'd have to kill you," refers to the quote from Maverick, "It's classified. I could tell you, but then I'd have to kill you."

". . . [B]ut first it's time to buzz the tower, and I'm not sorry about it . . ." refers to Maverick's line, "Sorry, Goose, but it's time to buzz the tower."

". . . [B]ecause I feel the need, the need . . . for speed," refers to Maverick saying to Goose, "I feel the need," and Goose finishing it off with, "the need . . . for speed."

"Don't tell me this isn't a good idea . . ." refers to Goose telling Maverick, "No, no, Mav, this is not a good idea," when Maverick wants to buzz the tower.

". . . I'm not a problem . . ." refers to Maverick asking Kazanksy, "What's your problem, Kazansky?" to which Iceman responds, "You're everyone's problem. . . ."

". . . [M]y ego's writing checks it *can* cash, son," refers to Stinger telling Maverick, "Son, your ego is writing checks your body can't cash."

"Altitude is dropping quickly. Speed leveling out, but it's too low. Up! Up! Speed Up! Up! Up! 'I'M TRYING TO GO UP!!!,' I shout. Speed Up! Up! Up! Speed Up! Speed increasing . . . shit! Too high now! Speed Down! Left! Left! Speed Down! Right! Right! Speed dropping, but, dammit, now it's too low! Up! Up! Speed Up! Up! Up!" refers to the on-radar screen commands to "guide" the player onto landing on the aircraft carrier. It is definitely not an easy *Top Gun* task, and it is one with very finicky controls to get correct the altitude and angle of the plane.

Level 8: Castlevania

"I shall sic on them my vile forces to inflict harm, and punishment my curse is," refers to *Castlevania III: Dracula's Curse*, which is the prequel to the first two NES *Castlevania* games. This poem follows the three NES *Castlevania* games in chronological order of in-game years, not in series order or when the games were released. Thus, the poem follows *III*, *I*, then *II*.

"Sacrificing their own, spiders descend from the skies," refers to the spiders in *Castlevania III* using smaller spiders (presumably their offspring) as their projectile weapons. In *Castlevania II* the spiders shoot webs instead of spiders.

"Stalking mummies reanimated by an evil spirit," refers to the two-mummy boss who is brought out of the coffin when the flaming spirit face drops into their coffin.

"Men engulfed in flames, blaze ground in a wake of fire," refers to the Fireman enemy that, after walking, leaves behind a trail of fire.

“Fire and ice from a companion freed, my minions abandon and concede,” refers to Syfa [also spelled Sypha] who is freed by Trevor then allowed to join him. She is a female vampire hunter who uses fire and ice magic projectiles.

“In a graveyard, a pile of bones resurrected,” refers to the Skull Knight boss that appears as just a shield on the ground until Trevor approaches, then it comes to life as a skeleton knight.

“A doctor’s monster no longer seeks affection,” refers to the boss of Dr. Frankenstein’s Monster, who, as the story goes, first sought affection upon being given life, but comes to inspire loathing in everyone who meets it.

“Two fire-breathing dragons spew forth flame,” refers to the Water Dragons boss.

“A demonic bone dragon, chased away, now in frame,” refers to the Bone Dragon King boss that Trevor fights. Reducing its health to a certain point causes it to leave the screen; it comes back elsewhere for Trevor to finish the battle.

“A half-breed child, my hunter’s adversary,” refers to the boss, Alucard, that Trevor fights.

“In defeat an offer to align, now matters vary,” refers to when Trevor beats Alucard, Alucard asks if Trevor would like for him to join.

“My flesh and blood, half human, half me . . .” refers to Alucard being Dracula’s half human / half vampire son.

“I gave you my name—it, you rearranged. Traitor, how can this be?” refers to the name Alucard—which is Dracula spelled backwards—and his offer to join with Trevor to kill Dracula. When a word whose spelling is derived from reversing the spelling of another word, is spelled backwards, it is a special type of anagram called an anadrome.

“My many faces of death: stalking, taunting,” refers to Dracula’s second form as a five-faced creature who drips blood for its attack as it moves around the screen.

"Ungodly winged beast, true form revealed, energy bolts my defense," refers to Dracula's third and final form.

"Will I return a century hence?" refers to the story of Dracula and how he returns every one hundred years due to the power of Christ weakening every century.

"But the Evil Count's impending doom is of no concern," refers to Dracula's larger plan of being killed by Simon. In doing so, he's sacrificing himself to place a curse on Simon, and that leads into . . .

"Him cowering in the corner, I can't attack, by design," refers to positioning Simon all the way to the left where the winged beast Dracula form cannot harm Simon. He can only jump up over Simon, and doing so redirects him off the wall to land back where he started, allowing Simon to chain whip Dracula when he lands. For the purposes of the poem, Dracula must lose this battle so that he can curse Simon. Therefore, he's attacking Simon in a manner that can't do any damage because Dracula must lose this fight.

"One final whip makes my demise, part of a larger plan to place a curse upon him and his clan," refers to the story of Dracula placing a curse on Simon Belmont at the conclusion of the final battle in *Castlevania*. Consequently, the story of *Castlevania II: Simon's Quest* is his quest to break the curse.

"'What a horrible night to have a curse,'" refers to the saying that appears on the screen when day transitions to night in *Castlevania II*.

"Ghosts and ghouls go from bad to worse," refers to the enemies being stronger and harder to kill when fought at night in *Castlevania II*.

"'The morning sun has vanquished the horrible night,'" refers to the saying that appears on the screen when night transitions to day in *Castlevania II*.

"The crack of the Vampire Killer, a sound to its handler's delight," refers to Simon's first whip, which is called the Vampire Killer.

"Acrid water holy burns bright, secrets made clear," refers to using holy water to burn wall and floor blocks, revealing new paths and books. These books contain secrets and tips to aid the player.

"With a strike of the stake, a symbol of evil will appaer," refers to one book found in Berkeley Mansion that reads, "A symbol of evil will app***ae***r when you strike the stake."

"A crystal bought white, bartered for blue then red," refers to purchasing a white crystal in the town of Jova and subsequently trading it for a blue crystal in the town of Aljiba, then finally exchanging the blue crystal for a red one in the town of Aldra.

"   ,Kneel to view ways that otherwise mislead," refers to a hidden book that reads, "to replenish earth ,kneel by the lake with the blue crystal." The spacing of the on-screen text is bad. Regarding the crystals' functions: the white crystal makes platforms visible; the blue crystal enables passage between lakes; and the red crystal allows passage between lakes and Deborah Cliff.

"Hidden books provide secrets and clues to be read," refers to the hidden books scattered throughout the game that offer valuable information for progressing, finding items, defeating bosses, and more.

"Aromatic leaves allow passage through lakes of dead," refers to laurels, which provide temporary invincibility and enable Simon to travel through poisoned marsh. "'Garlic in the graveyard summons a stranger,'" refers to a hidden book clue that informs the player to use garlic in the cemeteries to summon a gypsy.

"A requested gypsy offers a knife," refers to getting the Silver Knife from the Camilla Cemetery gypsy. It can be thrown farther than the dagger.

"Garlic in the mansion presents a danger," refers to using garlic to harm enemies.

"A requested gypsy gifts a bag of life," refers to obtaining the silk bag from the gypsy, which allows Simon to carry eight laurels instead of four. Laurels provide temporary invincibility, thus protecting life.

"Invest in an oak stake?" refers to the in-mansion merchant asking Simon if he wants to buy an oak stake. The oak stake is required to unlock the protective barrier around Dracula's body part. It's repeated in the poem because it pops up in every mansion. The first "Invest in an oak stake?" is written with a question mark because that is how it is presented by the merchant. As a player, you figure out you must have the oak stake to break the force field around the bag that holds the body part. So, going forward, it's no longer a question to buy, but a must to buy, thus, the next uses are with a period: "Invest in an oak stake."

"I shield you with my rib to take," refers to Dracula's rib found in Berkley Mansion. It can be used as a shield to deflect fireballs.

"My heart, passage the ferryman will make," refers to Dracula's heart found in Rover Mansion. Presenting the heart to the ferryman will make him take Simon to Brahm's Mansion.

"See with my eye through walls fake," refers to Dracula's eyeball found in Brahm's Mansion, which allows Simon to see objects hidden in fake walls.

"The strength of my nail gives power to break," refers to Dracula's nail found in Bodley Mansion, which allows Simon the power to break certain walls with his whip.

"Power to make evil burn awake is offered kneeling by the lake," refers to kneeling by the lake west of Bodley Mansion with the red crystal so that Simon can descend below to find the hidden soul who will trade Simon's Morning Star whip for the Flame Whip, doubling his attack power. "Awake" is stretched reference to "Morning [Star]."

"A disembodied face sheds tears of ache," refers to the floating face of Camilla (also known as Carmilla in other Castlevania lore) in Laruba Mansion, who uses bloody tears as an attack. "Ache" references tears stemming from pain or sadness, while bloody could suggest tears from a wound that hurts or aches (maybe).

"A golden dagger freezing in its wake," refers to the floating and moving face of Camilla stopping when hit with the dagger, allowing Simon to then whip it.

"In defeat, a magic cross for your sake," refers to beating Camilla and receiving the Magic Cross as a reward. It is required to access Dracula's castle.

"Steal my ring, entrance to my castle? Your access, I cannot forsake," refers to Dracula's ring found in Laruba Mansion. This ring is needed for Simon to enter Castlevania. Unlike the other body parts that provide additional functions, the ring does not serve any other purpose. It is solely required, along with the Magic Cross and the other body parts, to access Dracula's castle.

"A desolate path upon which my assassin snakes," refers to the absence of enemies in Dracula's castle as Simon snakes his way through to Dracula's lair.

"Rib, heart, eyeball, nail, and ring bakes," refers to Simon coming upon the brazier where he places Dracula's artifacts. They combust to form Dracula.

"With flame so sacred, a formidable foe I do not make," refers to the ease with which this version of Dracula can be defeated. He has the same hit points as Camilla, and he doesn't transform into a different being, which would prolong the fight or add more rounds to it. He is easily vanquished with the Sacred Flame.

"With skies red, the earth shall tremble and shake," refers to Ending One (below); "With skies clear, sense the text does not make," refers to Ending Two; "With skies gray, wounds prove fate, lacking haste, my killer's mistake," refers to Ending Three. All three lines refer to the different *Castlevania II* game endings. But the endings and related text don't make sense to each other.

Ending One (occurs when beating the game in seven

in-game days or less): Blood red sky. Simon stands in front of Dracula's gravestone, then bends down. The on-screen text reads, "The encounter with Dracula is terminated. Simon Belmont has put an end to the eternal darkness in Transylvania. His blood and sweat have penetrated the earth and will induce magic & happiness for those who walk on this land." The scene fades to darkness, Simon is gone, and night falls. The gravestone violently trembles, then a human hand with a touch of blood on it emerges from the ground.

Ending Two (occurs when beating the game in eight to fourteen in-game days): Tranquil blue sky. Simon stands in front of Dracula's gravestone, then bends down. The on-screen text reads, "Although the confrontation between Simon and Dracula has concluded Simon couldn't survive his fatal wounds. Transylvania's only hope is a young man who will triumph over evil and rid the city of Dracula's deadly curse."

Ending Three (occurs when beating the game in fifteen in-game days or more): Gray skies. Simon is absent. The on-screen text reads, "The battle has consummated. Now peace and serenity have been restored to Transylvania and the people are free of Dracula's curse forever. And you, Simon Belmont, will always be remembered for your bravery and courage." No hand emerges from the ground. The gravestone reads, "Dracula, 1431 - 76."

The end-game onscreen text does not line up with the on-screen image:
Ending One should have the text from Ending Three.
Ending Two should have the text from Ending One.
Ending Three should have the text from Ending Two.

Level 9: The Legend of Zelda

The Legend of Zelda chapter was specifically chosen to be Level 9 because it references Level 9: Death Mountain / Spectacle Rock, which is the final level of my favorite NES game.

"It's dangerous to go alone. Fortunately, I took this with me . . ." refers to the Old Man at the beginning of *The Legend of Zelda* who offers Link the sword while saying, "It's dangerous to go alone! Take this."

"I didn't start with the sword; I found it," refers to *The Legend of Zelda* development team's decision to introduce players to its non-linear world by having them begin the game with no weapons. Instead, players must immediately explore and enter the first cave to find the sword.

"Despite visual proof to the contrary, I did not have another option," refers to the game's instruction manual screenshot. It shows how in the first cave, the Old Man offers Link the choice between the boomerang and the sword.

"Going up, left, down, and left again (I'm not lost) has led me through the woods . . ." refers to the route the player must take to navigate through the Lost Woods. Exiting the woods leads to the graveyard.

"I find something magical, but I don't have enough 'heart' to master it . . ." refers to finding the Old Man who denies Link the "magical sword" if the player hasn't obtained twelve heart containers. While commonly called the Master Sword, it is not called the Master Sword in *The Legend of Zelda*. However, the Old Man says, "Master using it and you can have this." Link needs to have twelve heart containers to obtain the Magical Sword.

". . . ([W]hich wasn't a problem with the last sword offered to me)," refers to only needing five heart containers to obtain the White Sword from the Old Man.

"I do have heart . . . but I know courage won't come until next time," refers to the Triforce of Courage being first mentioned in *Zelda II: The Adventure of Link*. While the Triforce of Power and Triforce of Wisdom are mentioned in *The Legend of Zelda*, the Triforce or Courage is introduced later in the series.

". . . [H]yped to rule this land . . ." refers to the land of Hyrule.

". . . [T]o be its hero," refers to the Link character often referred to as the Hero in Zelda lore. Upon rescuing Zelda, she tells him, "Thanks Link, you're the hero of Hyrule."

"Is that a donkey with swords for arms?" refers to the Lynel enemy, which has four legs, but the sword shooting creates the impression the sprite has swords for arms.

"Sometimes, I find secrets to everybody . . ." refers to encounters with the cave-dwelling Friendly Moblin, who famously quips, "It's a secret to everybody," when giving rupees to the player. Other encounters may involve a money-making game of chance or being told, "Pay me for the door repair charge."

"Word of advice: if you ever find an old man who offers you either a life potion or a heart . . . always take the heart," refers to those options. It's always best to take the heart container because it increases the player's overall health, and the player can always buy life potions but never heart containers.

"I'm just trying to climb stairs here, and a falling boulder violently crashes towards me. Unable to move laterally on the stairs, I'm hemmed in, and backtracking my climb is my only option to avoid the boulder of death . . . it didn't work," refers to Link's inability to move laterally when on stairs to avoid boulders, which makes it easy for him to get hit by the bounding boulders of Death Mountain.

"I stop, watch the enemies' movements as I clock their habits, but frozen in time, they make for easy kills," refers to the clock or stopwatch item that freezes all on-screen enemies, making it easier to defeat them.

"Speaking of skeletons, they're not good at hiding items," refers to being able to see a door key through the skeleton's body.

"I link up with the old man again; he hands me a letter to fill my heart with love [potion]," refers to getting the blue letter from the Old Man who instructs Link to, "Show this to the Old Woman." Doing so allows Link to buy blue and red life potions (blue for one use and red for two uses). Clearly, "link up," writes itself.

"I bargain shop for a bigger shield—boy, this is really expensive! But I shop around to find the cheapest price possible," refers to the three merchants who sell the big shield at different prices: 160, 130, and ninety rupees. The merchant's remark to Link, "Boy, this is really expensive," adds a bit of humor to Link's purchase.

"Arrows aren't cheap, either," refers to the cost of one rupee to shoot an arrow.

"I have to save up money for a ring. No, not for a princess, for me. I blue almost all my money finally buying it," refers to needing 250 rupees out of a maximum carry amount of 255 to purchase the Blue Ring. The Blue Ring increases Link's defense and changes his tunic color from green to blue.

"'You don't want none of this smoke,'" refers to the Old Man in Level 2 advising Link, "Dodongo dislikes smoke," indicating that Link should use bombs to beat him. However, Dodongo must eat the bombs.

"I battle on, finding good fortune (plus a raft) in one auspicious shaped dungeon," refers to the Level 3 dungeon shaped like a swastika. However, it is the Manji symbol in Buddhism that signifies the Buddha's footsteps and represents "good fortune." It is also used to denote Buddhist temples on Japanese maps. The symbol was appropriated by Hitler and Nazi Germany, leading to its auspicious presence in the game.

"I make use of my boomerang to pick up far away items, but not too far away," refers to the blue boomerang, which travels half the length of the screen. In contrast, the red boomerang ("Magical Boomerang") travels the full length.

"Something ate my new big shield . . . at least he was kind enough to spit out my old one. Like, like, why did you have to steal my shield?" refers to the very annoying enemy called "Like Like" that will eat Link's Magical Shield. Link will get back his smaller wooden shield, but the Magical Shield is gone for good until Link buys another one.

"I lean against a statue to rest; of course, it comes to life, but it's not all bad. I pair a bracelet with my ring, and I can feel its strength. Now you're playing with power, I say to myself," refers to pushing a specific Armos statue to reveal the Power Bracelet. The Power Bracelet allows Link to move rocks, which reveal warp access points. "Now you're playing with power," references the bracelet's name, but also was an advertising tag line used by Nintendo®.

"I dodge some bouncing mice-like creatures. I try yelling at them, but I'm not loud enough to scare them away . . . Maybe I should whistle at them," refers to being able to yell into the Famicom's second controller's microphone to scare the Pols Voice instantly killing all of them in a room. The Old Man's advice that Pols hate loud noises was taken to mean you could play the whistle/flute ("Maybe I should whistle at them . . .") in their presence to impact them. His advice was a relic from the Famicom version of the game that was not taken out of the NES version, so his advice was irrelevant and thus only confusing to the player.

"With all my might, I obtain the power to unlock any door," refers to Link obtaining the Magicical Key. Link can unlock any door now, and the on-screen key total switches from a number to the letter 'A,' which stands for almighty, not all or any key.

"Crossing rivers of blood . . ." refers to red streams in the game not being lava, but blood (blue streams are clearly water), according to "The Official Nintendo Player's Guide." "I'm told a secret, nay, a fairy good secret, about where they don't live," refers to the Old Man telling Link, "There are secrets where fairies don't live," in Level 6. The secret leads to the entrance to Level 7. Playing the flute causes the water to recede revealing the entrance to the level. "Nay" refers to the homonym ney, which is a Persian flute.

"Grumble, grumble . . . goes my stomach. I'm hungry, so I grab some grub but find a better use for it," refers to needing to purchase food to give to the Goriya in Level 7. Feeding him makes him disappear, so Link can pass.

"My heart is full, as is my head with the battle-hardened wisdom. I enter death—dark thoughts, I know—but I'm no shadow of myself (that will come in my next adventure . . . and I won't cower in the corner, though that confidence might make for an error, I'll have company). Will I make a spectacle of myself remains to be seen?" refers to Link having the max sixteen heart containers so that he can head to Spectacle Rock where he can bomb open the entrance to Level 9, ultimately where he will face Ganon. In

Level 8, the Old Man advises Link, "Spectacle rock is an entrance to death." "—[D]ark thoughts, I know—but I'm no shadow of myself (that will come in my next adventure . . . and I won't cower in the corner, though that confidence might make for an error, I'll have company)," refers to Link facing Dark Link at the end of *Zelda II: The Adventure of Link*. In the Great Palace, the final boss battle is a shadow of Link that jumps out of his being to face Link. It's a tough battle made effortless by Link ducking down in the left corner and slashing at Dark Link. Ducking in the corner, Link cannot be hit. ". . . [C]onfidence that might make for an error, I'll have company)," refers to the Ruto villager named "Error," who introduces himself as "I am Error," in *Zelda II*. At the time, it was believed to be a translation error, but that proved to be false.[12] If the player enters Spectacle Rock without all eight triforce pieces the player will be greeted with, "Ones who does not have triforce can't go in." ". . . [W]ith battle-hardened wisdom," refers to Link having to gather all eight units of the triforce *with* wisdom, which Princess Zelda divided and hid throughout Hyrule to keep away from Ganon before she was captured by him. Triforce with wisdom as it is referred to on the intro screen, it later comes to be called the Triforce of Wisdom. Whew, that was a lot unpack.

"I encounter my most formidable foe yet; one I must patranize repeatedly, so I map out a plan of attack," refers to the Patra mini-boss. It is one of the toughest foes in the game and one which Link encounters multiple times in Level 9. The Old Man tells Link, "Patra has the map."

"I ready myself with a new ring," refers to Link obtaining the red ring. The red ring increases Link's defense and changes his tunic color to red.

"A rrow of silver lines my quiver," refers to Link ob-

---

[12] Hofmann, C. (n.d.). What's Up with the "I Am Error" Guy in Zelda II? Legends of Localization. Retrieved February 9, 2024, from https://legendsoflocalization.com/whats-up-with-the-i-am-error-guy-in-zelda-ii/

taining the silver arrow. It is required to defeat Ganon.

"I can hear the beast a room over, eye must be getting close," refers to the Old Man telling Link, "Eyes of skull has a secret." The layout of Level 9 is shaped like a skull and the left eye on the map is where Link will rescue Princess Zelda.

"I try to force with power my sword into him . . ." refers to the Triforce with Power that Ganon holds (the intro screen reads, "Many years ago Prince Darkness "Gannon" stole one of the triforce with power."; triforce with Power as it is referred to on the intro screen, it later comes to be called the Triforce of Power.

"Now's my chance to ennd him, to end <u>thi</u>s quest." refers to the main story line being the first quest, and *The Legend of Zelda* offering a second quest after the conclusion of the first quest (or by inputting 'ZELDA' as the player's name). "To ennd him," refers to the Ganon name spelled with two 'n's in the intro screen when the story reads, "Many years ago Prince Darkness 'Gannon' stole one of the triforce with power. . . ." But subsequent references to his name spell it with only one 'n.'

Level 10: Kid Icarus

"And fire an arrow at a grim-looking man, hoping to reap some hearts, but he sees me and freaks out, siccing his minions on me. Nonetheless, I cash in," refers to the grim reaper enemy in *Kid Icarus* and his behavior upon seeing Pit. If Pit is behind the grim reaper, Pit can shoot him without issue. Additionally, when killing him or any other enemy, Pit can pick up hearts which serve as currency in this game.

"An evil snake woman has pitted me . . ." refers to, Pit, the hero of *Kid Icarus*.

". . . [T]o free a lady pal untenable to me," refers to Lady Palutena, whom Pit is trying to rescue.

"I harp on the fact that I can play a tune to turn my enemies into mallets," refers to Pit getting the harp, an item that can turn all on-screen enemies into mallets.

"Being selective with my shots is a skill," refers to the consequence of losing skill points every time Pit fires an arrow. Skill points are necessary to participate in the endurance chambers, where Pit can receive arrow power-ups.

"I have a nose to find a chamber a different route would have hidden, in it (although with large hearts) bespectacled flying foes have bad intentions," refers to the necessity of climbing on the left to access a chamber with Specknoses in level 1 - 1 of the game. If the player climbs to the right, s/he will be unable to access the chamber due to the game's lack of backtracking. Specknoses drop large hearts worth ten hearts.

"I drink from the floating chalice of life when I feel low," refers to the random goblet suspended in the air for the player to grab, which refills one bar of health.

"From left to right / right to left I go to make my climb," refers to Pit's unique ability in the vertical progression stages to traverse off-screen on the left and reappear on the right side, and vice versa, a feature not commonly found in NES games.

"I pay to play a treasure game, winning a single feather. Huh?" refers to the treasure guessing-game where the player can win an item upon successful completion. In *Kid Icarus*, the purpose of items like feathers was often unclear (at least to a young me).

"I try intimidating the storekeeper. I'm no angel even in this land (but really, I am), but I can't win because I'm not strong enough; I go on," refers to being able to intimidate the storekeeper to lower his prices if Pit already has a strength upgrade, if not, the store owner will raise his prices. In regular shops (not black-market ones) the player can press 'A' + 'B' at the same time on a second controller, and that will cause Pit to intimidate the store owner. If it works, the text will change to, "I guess I can't win!" and then the prices drop. "Go on? Who do you think I am?" is said by a shop owner that is not intimidated, and then he raises his prices. The regular shops greet Pit with, "May I help you? We have everything." The black-market shops greet Pit with, "What do ya say! Try buying from me." The prices will lower as long as Pit's strength is one level higher than the number of the world Pit is in. "I'm no angel even in this land," refers to Pit being an angel in Angel Land.

"I barrel my way through, not losing my bottle for life, but in my haste, I fall off a platform from where I just jumped. Fortunately, I'm light as a feather . . . 'I'm Finished,' I am not," refers to being able to buy a barrel to hold extra life potions (up to eight). In British slang, 'he bottled it' or 'he lost his bottle' means to lose one's courage. If Pit possesses a feather when he falls off a platform with nothing below him, the feather will briefly lift him back up. If Pit dies, the screen reads, "I'm Finished." "I fall off a platform from where I just jumped," refers to the vertical stages where, if a platform goes off the screen, Pit will die if he fell instead of the screen dropping down and Pit landing on the platform right below where he once was.

"A group of four flying eyeballs dive at me; I duck, avoiding them, then fire upon their half-hearted attempt to hit me," refers to the Monoeye enemies that swoop down and try to hit Pit. Killing them leave behind a half-heart, which is worth five hearts.

"Winged nuisances fall from above; they recoil at the sight of my arrow and soon become hissstory," refers to the Shemum enemy, which is a winged snake in *Kid Icarus*, accompanied by a couple of snake puns.

"I played another treasure game and, to my credit, came away with a nice prize," refers to the possibility of winning the credit card in the treasure game. The credit card allows the player to buy items at the black market without having enough hearts/currency. However, future hearts collected will be used to pay off the debt incurred from these purchases.

"After enduring training, it was such an outstanding performance that I took a (sacred) bow," refers to completing the first sacred training chamber and being able to choose your reward: flaming arrows, crystal rod (for protection) or the sacred bow.

"I'm no weakling, look how much farther I can shoot," refers to failing the endurance training or leaving the room before it's over and Pit being met with, "You weakling!" The sacred bow allows Pit to shoot arrows farther.

"Another chamber: I'm skilled enough to take what made him glad I came," refers to having enough skills points that when Pit enters it, the chamber is not empty (which would be the case if Pit doesn't have enough skill points). In this chamber Pit is met with a bald Jesus-looking figure who says, "Glad you came Pit, here, take this." Pit receives an arrow upgrade, increasing his hit damage from one to two.

"I select a mallet and sober up some stoned archers," refers to pressing 'select' on the controller to switch to the mallet, which Pit uses to hit the centurions who have been turned to stone. These centurions aid Pit in the boss battles, but they're mostly ineffective and die quickly. "An empty hospital is of no use to me," refers to finding the hospital room in the fortress. If Pit is cursed with eggplant head, then this is where it is removed. However, if he isn't cursed, then nothing happens in the hospital room.

"I come to a room with a pit of yellow . . . something: lava, acid, piss; I don't know. Déjà vu. . . . This seems familiar to me, in fact elements of this world and some of its enemies I think I've seen before. I had good luck last time I dove into a pit of yellow, so here I go again," refers to how *Kid Icarus* shares similarities with *Metroid*, as both games were developed by many of the same NES game design team members. *Kid Icarus* has a linear stage progression unlike *Metroid*, but both games feature similar visual aesthetics, including the yellow liquid pit, same level design elements and clearly metroids are found in *Kid Icarus* towards the end of the game.

"Déjà vu . . . as to why: hard solving for an ace detective, let alone me," refers to the protagonist Ace Harding, from *Déjà Vu*. Ace was framed for murder, and the gameplay is about Ace clearing his name.

"Hot damn! I spring up with renewed health," refers to the yellow pit, which acts as a hot spring that restores Pit's health.

"One final arrow for t' win, and the beast bellows in pain," refers to the Twinbellows boss in the first fortress.

"A bounding thief comes for my hard-earned possessions. My bow is useless against him, so I stay grounded and slide under his jump, avoiding his sticky fingers," refers to the enemy, Pluton. Pluton cannot be killed and will steal any attack or defensive upgrades Pit has obtained. If Pit wants to reclaim the stolen item, he must buy it back on the black market for a hefty price.

"I briefly grazed some lava, but I was quick enough not to take any damage (surprisingly, water instantly kills me), nor was the lava's heat intense enough to make me melt," refers to being able to quickly jump in and out of lava without any health damage, but falling into water is an instant death. ". . . [M]ake me melt," refers to the story of Icarus' wax wings.

"I find a map, I check it, but it's useless; pencil me in for torching this thing the first chance I get," refers to the player obtaining a map (referred to as a check sheet) that is useless unless s/he has a pencil and/or torch. The pencil allows the player to mark visited rooms on the map (rooms will be colored differently on the map). The torch helps the player determine his/her location on the map.

"Arrows firing, by my mighty darts the beast hewn, draw back my bow, and I release one last volley," refers to Hewdraw, the Hydra-like boss in fortress two.

"I treasure my ability to make light work with my arrows," refers to receiving the Arrow of Light for defeating Hewdraw.

"A familiar enemy, a jellyfish appearance with sharp penetrating fangs, dives at me. I have bad memories of these, but I can't place where and why," refers to encountering the metroid-looking enemy near the end of *Kid Icarus*. The reasoning for this is explained above in the yellow pit section.

"As I slay the final beast, a blob-like creature, I don't know what box I've opened," refers to defeating the boss named Pandora (as in Pandora's Box) of world 3 - 4 in *Kid Icarus*.

"Him, with arrows, I peg, as suspected, wings I receive," refers to defeating Pandora and being rewarded with the Pegasus Wings.

"I fly, and I fly, and I fly, but I fall . . . I'm far from the sun, but I'm still a son, never to be an adult . . ." refers to the final stage—the Medusa stage—where Pit equips his three treasures, one being the Pegasus Wings, allowing him to fly. ". . . I'm far from the sun . . ." alludes to the story of Icarus, who tried to escape his captor by flying away with his wings of wax and feathers. Not heeding his father's warning, he flew too close to the sun, and it melted the wax sending him plunging to his death. ". . . [B]ut I'm still a son, never to be an adult . . ." refers to the multiple endings of *Kid Icarus*. Depending on various factors, Lady Palutena may turn Pit into an adult, but two endings keep Pit as a child.

"A dilemma deduced sadly by me . . ." refers to Medusa, the primary antagonist in *Kid Icarus*. She is responsible for turning Lade Palutena into a stone statue and spreading chaos throughout Angel Land.

". . . I am a forgotten hero," refers to the fact that, despite the game's popularity on the NES, the *Kid Icarus* franchise did not continue on future consoles like other well-liked NES franchises that appeared on SNES, Nintendo 64, and GameCube. Unbeknownst to me, the second installment of the *Kid Icarus* franchise was released on the Game Boy Advance in 1991, and (known to me) *Kid Icarus: Uprising* was released for the Nintendo® 3DS in 2012.

Level 11: Contra & Gradius

"Destroyed the vile red falcon and saved the universe; consider yourself a hero, I'm told," refers to the *Contra* end screen that reads, "Congratulations! You've destroyed the vile red falcon and saved the universe. Consider yourself a hero."

". . . ([N]ow, I am recognized) . . ." is a callback to the forgotten hero in the *Kid Icarus* level.

". . . I'm like a vicious viper waiting to strike . . ." refers to the ship's name, Vic Viper.

"Once again, my nemesis . . ." refers to the planet Nemesis that Vic Vaper is on, as well as the arcade version of *Gradius*, which was initially released internationally outside Japan under the title *Nemesis*.

". . . [A] big core belief of mine is to fire upon anything impeding my progress, but this time it's different . . ." refers to the end stage boss, Big Core, which Vic Viper faces five times throughout *Gradius*.

". . . [W]ith my finger off the trigger, I dodge and

move, slipping between its beams," refers to the ability to avoid Big Core's beam attack without needing to fire upon it; eventually it will self-destruct.

"Dodging giant ring shooting statues, all head no body, I head east—err, is landing this ship an option or what?" refers to the Easter Island looking statues that fire beams from their mouths.

"Efficiently, I make quick work of a squadron of ships by baiting them up and down, I'd love to open fire, but I must show restraint, 'mother . . . !' and I chill, drawing from my past to stick and move," refers to the Mother and Child enemy; the approach is to just dodge its attack. ". . . [D]rawing from my past experiences to stick and move" is a callback to the *Mike Tyson's Punch-Out!!* level where Doc's advice to Little Mac is to "stick and move, stick and move!"

"Gradiually, I use . . ." refers to *Gradius*.

". . . [D]on't mind me and I won't be bothered by you . . ." refers to the final boss, a brain, and how it is easy to defeat because it has no attacks.

". . . ([H]ave we met before?) . . ." is a callback to facing the final boss, Mother Brain, in the *Metroid* level.

". . . [A] life forced from salvation meanders across space and time," refers to the NES game *Life Force*, which was released as a spin-off to *Gradius*. The arcade version of *Gradius*, which predated the NES game, was called *Salamander* ("sal . . . meanders . . .") in Japan.

". . . I was the first, not t*he*y who came before me," refers to how the Konami Code's first appearance was in *Gradius*. While popular belief suggests the code first appeared in *Contra*, it was more colloquially known as the "Contra Code" during the NES days. Only as its popularity grew and it became more prevalent did it get recognized as the Konami Code.[13] ". . . [N]ot they who came before me,"

---

[13] DMarket. (n.d.). Cracking the Konami Code. DMarket Blog. Retrieved February 9, 2024, from https://dmarket.com/blog/cracking-konami-code/

refers to the beginning of this level: "t*he*y" being two people playing cooperative *Contra*; "he" being single player *Contra*.

Each sentence of the first section begins with the corresponding input of the Konami Code. The first letter of each sentence of the final section spells K-O-N-A-M-I C-O-D-E G-R-A-D-I-U-S.

Final Level / Boss Battle

"Duh nuh nuh nuh nun na," refers to the *Super Mario Bros.* castle world music.

"It's quite an estate they have here. There were many obstacles along the way (what an adventure) that were overcome by me . . . and by you, bil-leeee-v-me [said in my best Louisiana Creole drawl]," refers to *The Adventures of Bayou Billy*. The beginning of the game shows Godfather Gordon, who has kidnapped Billy's girlfriend, Annabelle. He says to Billy, "I'm taking Annabelle away. If you want her back. You will have to come to my estate. You will find that before reaching my estate there will be many obstacles to overcome. Let's see if you have what it takes to get there."

"An intricate design showcases a collection of shapes, patterns, and blocks . . . but it is a design that feels unfinished . . ." refers to *Tetris* and the puzzle aspect of fitting pieces into the design.

"The artwork unveils differing collections of cool or warm colors depending on the sunlight's reflection," refers to the *Tetris* puzzle pieces changing colors as a player progresses to a new level.

"Built of only four distinct shapes: straight, square, L, and zigzag . . ." refers to four puzzle piece shapes.

". . . [T]hey combine into an interlocking quartet rising . . ." refers directly to *Tetris*.

". . . [B]ut its ascent does so cautiously, as if mindful not to rise too high," refers to *Tetris*' puzzle-building dynamic, where the stack must not breach the board's top to avoid ending the game.

". . . I have concluded: so be it; a mind game it is," refers to the NES box cover art tagline for *Tetris*, "The Soviet Mind Game."

"The sun is angry today, my friends. I've heard of the man on the moon, but if I squint, I can almost see the scowl on the sun's face," refers to the fiery menace from *Super Mario Bros. 3*, relentlessly chasing Mario in the World 2 desert level.

". . . [I]s a dreamscape of a garden abundant with sprouts, turnips, onions, beets, radishes . . . and a cherry tree . . ." refers to the vegetables *Super Mario Bros. 2* that Mario can pull from the ground to use as projectiles. "[D]reamscape" refers to the idea of the game being just a dream, or the events took place, and the dream is Mario's mind recreating the events with his memories . . . or something entirely different.[14]

"To the cherry tree for five seconds, I intently stare, manifesting . . ." refers to some stages in *Super Mario Bros. 2* having cherries, and if the player collects five cherries in a row, it will make an invincibility Starman appear.

". . . [A] giant frog hopping . . . His entrance is thwarted . . ." refers to the main protagonist, Wart, in *Super Mario Bros. 2*. Wart is a fat regal frog.

---

[14] Marioverse Wiki. (n.d.). Theory: Super Mario Bros. 2 wasn't a dream. Retrieved March 22, 2024, from https://marioversewiki.com/wiki/Theory:_Super_Mario_Bros._2_wasn%27t_a_Dream

". . . [A] thick hedgerow of tall grass with a solitary tree in the distance. . . . At the foot of the tall grass, a basset hound sniffs around. Nose down, butt up, tail wagging frantically as he shoots around the clay ground. Suddenly, he leaps into the tall brush—he must have caught a scent of something—his big floppy black ears perking up as he jumps. Disappearing from my view, he startles up a couple of ducks moments later. One with a green head casually flies away, while a purple-headed one frantically darts to-and-fro," refers to elements of *Duck Hunt*. ". . . [S]hoots around the clay ground," refers to the option of choosing clay shooing at the start screen of *Duck Hunt*.

"I see another duck; he's purple as well, but he's different. He's a lot more animated, and his wings are a darker shade. Or is that a cape?" refers to Darkwing Duck, the Disney animated character featured in his own titular game. While Darkwing lacks wings, he sports a distinctive cape.

". . . [T]ells me to S.H.U.S.H. I suspect something F.O.W.L. is going on here . . ." refers to the undefined S.H.U.S.H. acronym (which also appears as SHUSH in the *Darkwing Duck* multiverse). S.H.U.S.H. is an international super-secret peacekeeping organization with an undisclosed acronym. F.O.W.L., on the other hand, stands for Fiendish Organization for World Larceny, which is a global crime syndicate and terrorist organization.

". . . [M]aybe it's just gas I smell," refers to Darkwing's gas gun that he uses to shoot enemies.

"A couple of heavy claps of thunder appear rowdy enough to provide cover for him to vanish into the shadows," refers to the gas gun upgrades available to Darkwing: heavy; thunder; arrow.

". . . I now notice another flock of feathered tales . . ." refers to *DuckTales.*

". . . [O]r possibly sugarcane. But scroo(ge) it . . ." refers to the character of Scrooge McDuck and his use of a cane as a weapon in *DuckTales*.

". . . [A]lthough I would like to tell you how cute each one is with his color-matched cap complementing his outfit," refers to Capcom, the Japanese video game company behind some terrific NES games and franchises such as *Mega Man*, as well as various licensed Disney games and others listed in the "Easter Eggs Explained" section.

"As I continue down the path, I stumble upon a collection of bikes piled near each other. Biking to work is common, but dirt bikes seem like an odd choice for transportation. A plume of smoke rises from one—looks like it over-heated," refers to *Excitebike*. The bike can overheat when the accelerator button is pressed past the maximum.

"Two cute little critters scurry across my path (one a bit chipper than the other). I nearly stepped on them; one hid under a box that acted as a shield, the other just backpedaled," refers to the chipmunk characters, Chip and Dale.

"Fortunately, I caught myself in time to alter my step so they wouldn't need rescuing from the stomping of my Ranger boots," refers to *Chip 'n Dale Rescue Rangers*.

". . . I can now discern outfits: the black-nosed one looks like a famous adventurer, while the red-nosed one resembles a detective or more like a private investigator," refers to how Chip—the black-nosed one—dresses like Indiana Jones, and Dale—the red-nosed one—dresses like Magnum, P.I.

". . . [L]urking in a sorta nook, I see a raccoon. Suited . . ." refers to the Tanooki Suit in *Super Mario Bros. 3*. The suit transforms Mario/Luigi into Tanooki Mario/Luigi. It is based on the Japanese mythological creatures inspired by Japanese raccoon dogs (tanuki) who can use leaves to shape-shift and cause chaos.[15]

[15] MarioWiki. (n.d.). Tanooki Suit. Retrieved March 16, 2024, from **https://www.mariowiki.com/Tanooki_Suit**

". . . [M]akes eye contact with me and freezes like a statue . . . he furiously whips his tail about to elevate himself off the ground," refers to the Tanooki Suit which grants the player the same flying, gliding, and tail-whipping abilities as the Super Leaf, but with the added ability to turn into a statue letting the player briefly hide from enemies and hazards.

"But not to be upstaged. . . . Is that play for him?" refers to the to-be-proven-true by Shigeru Miyamoto theory that *Super Mario Bros. 3* was a stage performance or play.

"Will his path to exit stay just right for him to escape . . ." refers to how Mario will exit stage right when most levels in *Super Mario Bros. 3* are completed.

". . . I see an overgrown man child topless in a grass skirt hurrying towards me, his feet moving a mile a minute?" refers to Master Higgins in *Adventure Island.*

". . . I wonder where that boy—err—man is off to?" refers to *Adventure Island*, which began its development as a direct port of the Sega arcade game *Wonder Boy*.[16]

"'Master,' he begins (he's close enough upon me now that I notice a milk mustache), 'which dock ta sail from?' Showing me a letter in his palm (a fistful of fruit in the other), 'Dis prints es teeny,'" refers to [stay with me on this one] the playable character, Master Higgins, who is trying to get to Adventure Island after hearing the Evil Witch Doctor kidnapped Princess Tina. In the game, Master Higgins consumes various fruits to replenish his health and drinks milk to refill his vitality meter.

"To a warmer ocean climate is a venture I land on . . ." refers to *Adventure Island*, which takes place on an island in the South Pacific.

". . . [B]ut I can't stop thinking about that letter. Maybe it had a hidden message on it he needed, or

---

[16] Fandom. (n.d.). Adventure Island (video game). Wonder Boy Wiki. Retrieved February 9, 2024, from https://wonderboy.fandom.com/wiki/Adventure_Island_(video_game)

maybe what he was looking for was written in the stars. In the tropics, where I've decided he's going, is where he'll find it. That reminds me of when my archaeologist uncle, Steve, sent me a letter (a stained letter, actually) from a long voyage in the islands. He was in the water—probably why I could tell the letter got wet before—on a boat, or maybe it was a sub. See—yo, yo, I'm talking to you here, pay attention!—if I have to go somewhere far, I'm taking a plane —something big—like a 747," refers to *StarTropics*. The physical game was packaged with a letter addressed to the playable character, Mike, from his Uncle Steve. In the game on-screen text from Dr. Jones' assistant reads that he must tell Mike Dr. Jones' last words, "Tell Mike to dip my letter in water. . . ." Dipping the letter in water reveals the hidden text: "Its frequency is 747MHz." The player inputs 747 in the frequency tracking system to operate Dr. Jones' 'Sub-C' submarine. This sets it on a course to Dr. Jones' last location. ". . . [Y]o, yo, I'm talking to you . . ." refers to Mike's primary weapon, the yo-yo.

"And now, coming my way is a skinny, bearded man in red skivvies hoisting a lance high above his head (are there more of him, I ponder)," refers to the main character, Arthur, in *Ghost 'n Goblins*.

"My thought shifts to go stand 'n go blend . . ." refers to *Ghost 'n Goblins*.

"Minding my own business, I abruptly get sucked over to my left, the gust of air pulling me in enough to lift me off the ground for a split second. As I drop, my left foot instinctively braces against the curb enough . . ." refers to the character Kirby in *Kirby's Adventure*.

"Sensing that I'm out of harm's way, I look back to see a puffy pink thing with rosy cheeks (Is he blushing? Maybe he's embarrassed?) . . ." refers to Kirby's look.

"I can see that he ate bits of little animals . . ." refers to 8-bit. The NES uses an 8-bit microprocessor for its CPU (central processing unit) and the term "8-bit" refers to the size of the data bus in the CPU, which determines the amount of information the CPU can handle at one time. In the case of the NES, this meant that the CPU could process data in 8-bit chunks, which limited the graphics and audio capabilities of the games. As a result, games for the NES are often referred to as 8-bit games due to the technical specifications of the console.[17]

"A set of stairs before me, I watch two turtles descend, one up near the top and another before it," refers to the end set of stairs in World 3 - 1 of *Super Mario Bros*. There, Mario can repeatedly jump on the second turtle ("the 'one up' near the top"), bouncing it against a stair to accumulate points. Enough points will lead to extra lives known as 1-ups.

". . . I pass a flagpole as I approach the entrance," refers to the flagpole Mario jumps on at the conclusion of each non - 4 world in *Super Mario Bros.*

"The façade is covered in ivy or maybe vines, some shooting so high into the sky that it's as if they could reach the clouds," refers to the hidden vines in the *Super Mario Bros.* Worlds 2 - 1, 3 - 1, 5 - 2, 6 - 2. When the block holding the vine is struck, it grows up allowing Mario to climb into a cloud area to collect a bunch of coins.

"Off in the distance, I catch a glimpse of a meteorite shooting across the sky . . ." refers to the meteorite scene that opens *Maniac Mansion*.

". . . [O]n a welcome sign posted before the door. It greets me: WARNING!! TRESPASSERS WILL BE HORRIBLY MUTILATED," refers to the sign outside of the mansion in *Maniac Mansion.*

"I think about my situation for a second and what brought me here, 'Should this man shun this interview?' Reasons are many . . . 'Ack,' I say out loud . . ." refers to *Maniac Mansion*.

---

[17] Quora. (n.d.). Why are old NES games called as 8-bit games. Retrieved February 9, 2024, from https://www.quora.com/Why-are-old-NES-games-called-as-8-bit-games

". . . I'm at this point and [clicking is the sound made by the door handle as I turn it] I'm not trespassing," refers to *Maniac Mansion* being one of the first and few Nintendo® "point and click" games. Previous generations of games used a command line prompt, but *Maniac Mansion* took the command line prompt and streamlined it with the point-and-click feature. This made it more intuitive to play.

"Over to the right, around the corner, I see two brothers, twins: one toe-headed, the other chestnut, getting ready to duke it out with some high school kids. But these kids mean business. They're ruthless. Equipped with brass knuckles and lead pipes, they come out swinging. One brother throws an oil barrel, and the other pulls out a whip," refers to elements of *Double Dragon* and its twin brother characters, William "Billy" and James "Jimmy" Lee, and to elements of *River City Ransom* and its two high school characters, Alex and Ryan.

". . . [W]hile his buddy stones his foe with fast hands," refers to the fighting technique called "Stone Hands," which can be purchased in *River City Ransom.*

"On the foe's chin, a small river of blood comes to sit; teeth gritted, he ran some interference . . ." refers to the *River City Ransom*.

"([W]hat a slick move)," refers to the final boss, called "Slick," in the *River City Ransom* ransom letter, but his name is Simon.

"[I haven't seen fighting like this since that hockey game I attended. And that was in the stands, not on the ice, when some knucklehead with a switchblade steeling beers from other fans incited a brawl]," refers to *Blades of Steel,* which was famous for its on-ice fights.

"The thrashing was so hard that he dropped his lunch money . . ." refers to foes in *River City Ransom* dropping coins that Alex and Ryan can pick up to increase their money total. Money allows them to restore health and buy power ups, fighting techniques, and other items.

". . . [T]he blast's concussion elicited a barf response from the other," refers to enemies in *River City Ransom* often saying, "BARF" after getting hit in the face.

". . . [A] tiny-footed bystander practicing martial arts is waddling off like he just shat his pants . . . behind him, a trail of bees gives chase. In his hand, the pants portion of his sleeveless white (well, no longer) karate gi is klung. Fun times," refers to *Kung Fu* and how the character (who has very small feet) walks like he has a load in his pants. The challenging mini-boss on level four throws bees at the player. Fun fact: the player can decapitate the mini-boss with kicks to his head, but out of a cloud of smoke, he will regenerate with said head reattached.

"'Hey buddy,' a bleached-blonde kid in a tailored suit yaps at me, 'you wanna get a little action in on this?' Smacking a rolled-up newspaper against his palm, he's leaning against the wall. Streetwise, I am not . . ." refers to *Wall Street Kid*. In the game, the player can read the "Wall Street Times" for stock tips and other information.

"'You interested in buyin' a boat? What about a girlfriend . . . I bet you don't know I own a castle. Have you met my uncle, Mr. Benedict?'" refers to elements and storylines of *Wall Street Kid*.

"'She's a bit of a prima donna . . . I think you can *precisely* put a price on love,'" refers to Wall Street Kid's girlfriend, Prisila, the Pricey Prima Donna. Much of the game revolves around making money to purchase luxury items and other expensive things for her.

"'Have you seen my barometer around here?'" refers to the odd desk item choice in Wall Street Kid's office. The barometer allows Wall Street Kid to "get a list of exercises you can perform in order to maintain your healthy physique. Remember, if you don't watch yourself, you could end up too ill to do business. But don't overdo it, because exercise takes time away from doing business."

"'Should I short Yapple?'" refers to selling shares of

Apple stock. The strategy works when the price decreases, allowing for profits to be generated by selling it at a higher price first and then buying it back at a lower price. Shorting a stock is riskier than buying it because the downside is limited to $0 on a purchase. However, when a person shorts a stock, the downside risk is unlimited because the stock price can theoretically increase infinitely. It would not have been a wise long-term move for the Wall Street Kid since Apple stock was trading for pennies in the 1980s and is $180 per share at the time of this writing.

"'No matter what, do not . . . waste your time . . . with the carnival,'" refers to offering to take Prisila to the carnival always being answered, "Sorry honey, I'd get sick if I went on any rides today." But the "Wall Street Times" informs the reader, "Equipment failures cause injuries at carnival."

"'Are we taking my Fairrari or yours?'" refers to the game's choice of cars to purchase: a Fairrari 328 for $50,000 or the BMV 750IL for $25,000 (~$141,000 and $70,000, respectively, in 2024 dollars). The game features a lot of knock-off company names. Names like "Rattel Toys" instead of "Mattel Toys," "Boing" instead of "Boeing," and "YBM" instead of "IBM" are some examples.

"'I just wrecked my 328 . . .'" is a callback to the 328 Twin Turbo from the *Rad Racer & Paperboy* level.

"I can tell you about the time me and Billy Ray Cupid shorted the shit outta frozen OJ futures," refers to the premise of the final scene of the 1983 film *Trading Places*, where Billy Ray Valentine (played by Eddie Murphy) is involved in a futures contract play with Louis Winthorpe (played by Dan Aykroyd) to short orange juice futures based on the data in a bogus government crop report.

"We really nuked 'em, those Duke brothers!" refers to, albeit a non-NES game, *Duke Nukem* (but *Duke Nukem 3D* was released on Nintendo 64). The Duke Brothers are the two main antagonists in Trading Places; they were financially ruined by Winthorpe and Valentine's orange juice futures scheme. The Duke name was too good to pass up for a *Duke Nukem* Easter egg.

"'Use it . . . or lose it,'" refers to the saying on the box cover for *Wall Street Kid*.

"'The password? Haaaa! That's your fatal step . . .'" refers to another fighting technique in *River City Ransom* called, "Fatal Steps."

"'. . . [I]t's thirty-two characters long . . .'" refers to *River City Ransom*'s extremely long password system of thirty-two characters.

"'. . . [B]ut smiles are free,'" refers to how you can purchase for free a smile in Hack's Chicken Shack in *River City Ransom*.

". . . [D]ouble trouble . . . not on a half pipe (the place must not have been able to get a permit to build one). Hoping to skate on by to . . ." refers to *Skate or Die 2: The Search for Double Trouble* and its plot. The local half-pipe is getting demolished because it was built without a permit, thus kicking off the game's plot. The player needs to obtain money, blueprints, and a building permit to rebuild a larger half-pipe, now called "Double Trouble."

". . . [T]rouble on the double, drag on no longer will this fight, because suddenly everyone is distracted," refers to *Double Dragon*.

"'By George' . . . up the ramp a giant ape-like creature," refers to *Rampage* and the playable King Kong-like character named George.

"What kind of vitamins has this guy been taking?" refers to the Select Mutant screen in *Rampage,* where George is described as having "[e]ver growing concern over mega-vitamin."

"Out of the corner of my eye, I notice some armed green men behaving like teenagers, each with a bandana colored bright—not muted—in-to an open sewer hole they ninmbly jam and turn 'til they're out of sight," refers to

Teenage Mutant Ninja Turtles.

"Cowering, a bunch gone," refers to the Teenage Mutant Ninja Turtles' popular catchphrase, "Cowabunga."

"Meanwhile, other green men hop on hoverbikes and speed off, avoiding barriers along the way (well, trying to, at least, but they're not too successful at it)," refers to *Battletoads* (hop—pun intended) with a reference to the extremely hard "Turbo Tunnel" level.

"Suddenly, a flash of purple draws my attention away from the giant ape. With his sword sheathed and ready at the hip, a man bounces through the alley, spin-jumping onto a sign several feet above his head. He barely grazes it, and then in a flash, he's on top of the roof (knocking down a lantern in doing so . . . but I don't think it was accidental)," refers to elements of *Ninja Gaiden*.

"'Walter?' he breathes, his voice muffled, with an air of revenge about it," refers to the character, Ryu, in *Ninja Gaiden*, seeking out the archaeologist, Walter Smith, in response to his father's death. ". . . [H]is voice muffled with an air of revenge about it," refers to Ryu's murdered father because Ryu speaks his name through the face covering part of his ninja-yoroi, which is the name for a ninja's uniform.

"'Hi ya, bu . . .' I trail off, 'say . . . how did you get up there?'" refers to Ryu's last name of Hayabusa.

"I have finally reached the entrance of the red and white building that houses the game design company known as FAM. I, completely confounded . . ." refers to Famicom/Famicon, which is the name for the NES, or Family Computer, in Japan. In English, the word is Famicom, but in Japanese, because Famicom is a shortening of Family Computer and computer is spelled with an "n," the name is Famicon.[18] Red and white are the colors of the Famicom/ Famicon system.

---

[18] NESFiles. (n.d.). NES Controller Collection - Is it Worth It? NESFiles Forums. Retrieved February 9, 2024, from https://www.nesfiles.com/Forums/Collecting/0/2290

". . . [E]xhausted myself from the quest," refers to the end screen in *Super Mario Bros*. reading, "Your quest is over."

". . . [A] new one lies before me . . ." refers to the *Super Mario Bros*. end screen reading, "We present you a new quest."

". . . [B]ut I'm here at 8:40 . . ." refers to World 8 - 4, which is the final level in *Super Mario Bros.* where the player needs to pass Bowser to save Princess Peach.

"By my calculation, I have six minutes and forty seconds until the whole world is about to change, but it might happen sooner . . . well, it must," refers to the time given to complete *Super Mario Bros.* World 8 - 4 (400 seconds), but one must beat the level before the time runs out.

"My hair is so tough to manage; should I have worn a hat?" refers to Mario's trademarked hat look because his creator, Shigeru Miyamoto, thought it was easier to animate a hat than a full head of hair.[19]

"A bowl of jellybeans . . . Next to it, a note reads: USE DIFFERENT FLAVORS TO . . . [blah blah blah—it's not worth the trouble]," refers to *A Boy and His Blob: Trouble on Bobolonia.*

"I crane my neck and see an entrance to a kitchen," refers to the designers of A Boy and His Blob, David Crane and Garry Kitchen.

"With a shock of purple hair, a pajama-clad little boy—couldn't be much higher than my knee—moseys over to me," refers to *Little Nemo: The Dream Master*.

"He is clutching a tiny car toy in his right hand. It must be his favorite because the micro racer is all beat up with not much sheen on it anymore," refers to *Micro Machines*.

"'Sir, real-ly, I dreams of candy,'" refers to the surreal dreams of Nemo, where he feeds candy to animals so

---

[19] The National Videogame Museum. (n.d.). Mario and Cappy. Retrieved March 21, 2024, from https://thenvm.org/objects/mario-and cappy/#:~:text=Mario%20was%20first%20featured%20in,all%20lead%20to%20this%20hat.

that he can ride or become them. Each animal possesses skills that aid Nemo in completing a level or objective.

"'More, more, more . . . feed us,'" refers to Morpheus. The purpose of the game is for Nemo to travel to Nightmare Land to rescue Morpheus, the King of Slumberland, from the evil Nightmare King.

"'My goal really is to find keys,'" refers to the Gorilla, one of the animals who aids Nemo in his quest to find a set number of keys per level, which allows him to unlock the door to access the next level.

"Whatchamacalit . . . ultimately, Sam. Son's on some stuff, I'll tell ya that. Ya know, rich kid problems, split personality thing. He's a good kid, but best to leave him alone and forget about him," refers to *Little Samson*. Considered one of the NES' most underrated games ("He's a good kid"), it quickly fell into obscurity because it arrived at the end of the NES era when newer consoles had already come to market. "Rich kid problems" refers to the game's status as a coveted cartridge among collectors due to its high game-play quality and limited availability. Its rarity, stemming from low sales upon its release ("leave him alone and forget about him"), elevates its value to one of the most expensive titles sought after by enthusiasts. "Split personality" refers to the ability at any point during the level to switch characters between Little Samson, a dragon, a golem, and a mouse.

"A large man in a purple tracksuit ominously stares at me . . . He's sitting down, slumped against the wall," refers to Jason from *Friday the 13th* and to how he appears when he has been defeated.

"I think I had the same outfit, but in hot pink and a much smaller size," is a callback to when the character was in the jogging training scene in *Mike Tyson's Punch-Out!!*

"For he's security," refers to Jason's surname of Voorhies.

"A blank expression on his face," refers to Jason wearing his trademark hockey mask.

"Is he dead? Nope, he's alive . . . very much alive!" refers to having to beat Jason three times in *Friday the 13th*. A common theme in Jason movie lore is thinking he's dead when he really isn't.

"I don't know why, but I feel nepotism got him the job" refers to Jason's mother, Pamela Voorhies, who is the killer in the first *Friday the 13th* movie. [*spoiler alert!*]

"He motions for me to take my sweater off. I oblige," refers to the sweater armor in *Friday the 13th* that Jason's mother drops after defeating her. It's a powerful armor, but only female characters can equip it.

"Well, what for? I'm not going to R.O.B. the place," refers to Nintendo's® Robotic Operating Buddy or R.O.B., which was a toy robot accessory for the NES. Known as the Family Computer Robot in Japan, its name was changed to R.O.B. in North America.

". . . [A] gyro might hit the spot right about now . . . their food will stack-up against any grease joint in the area," refers to the only two games in the NES Robotic Operating Buddy Series: *Gyromite* and *Stack-Up*.

"A black-bearded man with horn-rimmed glasses to match clumsily charges forward in his brown trench coat [a flash of light] as he zaps past me. His pink trench coat, the color of bubble gum, and shoes pitter-pattering about as he bounds up and down my way to warn me, 'Danger! Watch out for falling rocks.' Confused, he's got my attention now, so he goes on. 'Hey, got any of those black panther diamonds? What about some red balloons? I don't need ninety-nine of them—twenty will do. Have you seen King Dom? Any power drinks or roast chickens, huh?' 'I don't know, pal,' I spit out as he hastily trails off in his green trench coat. Quit playing detective with me. A bottle whips across, nearly hitting me." There is a lot to unpack here. This paragraph refers to *Gumshoe*. Detective Stevenson is on the case of the mafia boss, King Dom. King Dom has kidnapped Stevenson's daughter, Jennifer. An on-screen note to start the game reads, “I’ve got your daughter. Bring the 5 ‘black panther’ diamonds to me within 24 hours or else! Come alone.” Stevenson’s trench coat begins as brown, then turns pink, then green. In gameplay, he continually walks to the right, and the player uses the NES Zapper, or light gun, to shoot him, thus making him jump to avoid pitfalls and enemies and to collect items. Shooting (other than Stev-enson) will use a bullet, but collecting ballons will replenish bullets. If the player collects twenty ballons in a stage it will reveal a secret bonus area if completed before passing the section of the level that transitions into the bonus area. Ninety-nine red balloons is a music reference to the song “99 Red Balloons / 99 Luftballons” by Nena. In level one of *Gumshoe* there is an area of falling rocks that starts with a “Danger” sign. If the player shoots a Lucky Bird, it might turn into a roast chicken. Lastly, bottles are frequently thrown across the screen that can be shot.

“. . . [F]ind a floppy disk lying on the floor. I pick it up. As analyze it, a hi-tech-looking ninja strides my way,” refers to *Strider*. The object of the game is to find floppy discs to unlock other parts (levels) of the world to explore. The Blue Dragon space station serves as the game’s stage select screen whereby disks can be analyzed to unlock levels.

“I espy two mischievous-looking characters snickering in the corner. I’m not well-versed in mischief, so this bottle-throwing nonsense I can’t grasp why,” refers to *Spy vs. Spy* with “grasp why” being the second iteration of the word “spy.”

“Identical twins, I’m guessing. They have egg-shaped heads, exaggeratedly long pointy snouts, and large dark black eyes. The only difference between them is their outfits: one is dressed all in white, while the other is all in black. The only contrasting element is the band around each of their wide-brimmed hats, which matches his brother’s color,” refers to the characters in *Spy vs. Spy*.

“Diabolical toothy grins can’t mask their true intentions," refers to the "Spy" characters wearing masks that cover their entire heads, with only the eyes and a small portion of their mouths visible. In doing research for this book, I never knew they wore masks; I always thought they just had exaggerated cartoonish facial features.

"Would it be MAD of me to ask, 'Who threw that bottle?' But I don't want to rag on them," refers to *MAD Magazine*. The "Spy" characters originated from the long-running cartoon strip in *MAD Magazine*. Rag is another term for a magazine.

"I think they're after each other . . . maybe I wasn't their target," refers to how the "Spy" characters are always at war with each other.

"One is a fighter, the other a warrior . . ." refers to the main character in *Final Fantasy* starting off as a fighter class; the other being "warrior" refers to the only playable character in *Dragon Warrior.*

". . . [A]s their chronicling (however, one is far more versed at this) begins . . ." refers to the *Final Fantasy Chronicles* compilation game (released on PlayStation).

". . . [D]eep into the knight they will go (well, at least one will)," refers to the main character in *Final Fantasy* leveling up from fighter class to knight class. The only playable character in *Dragon Warrior* does not level up to a name-changing class.

"Blue begins, 'Seeing you in the light, I can tell battle has aged you.' 'Well, lucky for you, you haven't changed a bit,' Red snipes," refers to the fighter in *Final Fantasy* leveling up to knight class which changes his sprite's appearance.

"'He was metal! I couldn't kill him . . . and he ran from me, ya know!'" refers to the metal slimes in *Dragon Warrior*. Despite only having four hit points, they are exceedingly difficult to kill because of their incredibly high defense. While they offer a substantial amount of experience points, they often flee before the Hero can defeat them.

"'Pack!?!' Red shouts. 'Dost thou mean wolf singular!?! Since when have you had to face multiple enemies with your mano a mano combat style?' 'It's not too hard facing multiple enemies when you've got a team with you: thieves, monks, multi-colored mages, ninjas . . .'" refers to in *Final Fantasy*, battles involve a team approach with four different characters, whereas in *Dragon Warrior*, the Hero faces battles alone. But the team approach in *Final Fantasy* means the party can face teams of enemies, so Blue's retort makes for a moot point.

"'At least you don't have to share the gold and XP,'" refers to the shared distribution of gold and experience points (XP) among team members in *Final Fantasy*. In *Dragon Warrior* the Hero accumulates all gold and XP.

"'Remember you left your buddy stoned that one time . . .'" refers to when a team member in *Final Fantasy* is stoned meaning literally petrified, thereby unable to earn experience points (this effect also occurs when a team member is deceased). The remaining party members get to accumulate the absent party member's XP.

"'Listen, you know who this goes; you and me both have got to be selective with our turn-based attack system. Say it with me now: R P G—'" refers to the genre of game-play known as turn-based role-playing games. Originally, RPG games were more popular in Japan, but then this gameplay style was brought to North America with games like *Final Fantasy* and *Dragon Warrior*. Turn-based RPG refers to a style of turn-based attack system in games like *Final Fantasy* and *Dragon Warrior*, instead of the more common action-adventure RPG style in games like *The Legend of Zelda* and *Metroid* that featured more button smashing. While both involve strategy, turn-based has another layer to it.

"'. . . [T]hou hath maketh a fair point,'" refers to the use of Elizabethan English in *Dragon Warrior*. It helps to give the game a more medieval or fantastical feel, in line with its setting and themes.

"'Oh yeah, wizards. I loaded them up with some spell

they wanted—of course, it cost me. Nothing's free—well, plenty of free spells in your land—I asked them how's it goin'. I was advised to temper my expectations,'" refers to the temper spell in *Final Fantasy*, which originally did not work as intended; however, the bug was fixed in remade versions of *Final Fantasy* playable on other devices. The temper spell is designed to harden the weapon of a team member, increasing the amount of damage s/he can inflict. Unfortunately, in the original version of the game, the spell had no effect. Additionally, there were other game bugs that made magic spells ineffective, as well.

"'Hmm, purchasing magic must've been nice; I had to earn it . . . not free for me,'" refers to being able to purchase magic spells in *Final Fantasy,* while magic spells were earned from leveling up in *Dragon Warrior.*

"'Well, it must be nice to *earn* a heal spell right out of the gate,'" refers to getting the much-needed heal spell in *Dragon Warrior* once the player levels up to level three.

"'I have to buy one potion, and then buy one potion, and then . . . buy . . . one . . . potion. No buying in bulk in my land,'" refers to how potions had to be bought one at a time in *Final Fantasy*, preventing the player from purchasing in bulk, such as buying ten at once. Similarly, in *Dragon Warrior*, bulk purchases weren't possible either, although the necessity to load up on potions was not as much of a requirement.

"'Yeah, don't remind me of the chest of gold that never disappeared only to magically replenish itself,'" refers to the treasure chest room in Tantegel Castle. After unlocking the door to the area with the magic key, the player can open the chests. The first four chests disappear upon opening, but the fifth one remains, only to be refilled with gold again, allowing the player to easily harvest gold.

"Red lifts his mug up high . . . 'Whether it be experience points, levels, new weapons and armor, whatever, one thing we can both agree on is nobody, and I mean *nobody,* grinds . . . like us,'" refers to how NES RPG games require the player to perform the same action countless times to level up, compared to similar adventure/ story games like *The Legend of Zelda*, which are more linear and don't require as much repetition to strengthen or progress in the game.

". . . [S]imultaneously, they both sing, 'I ain't afraid of no ghost.' . . ." refers to the line in the *Ghostbusters* theme song.

"'. . . [L]ucky you not to deal with Warmech—AKA *Death Machine*— . . .'" refers to the infamous foe in *Final Fantasy*. It is the most powerful random encounter in the game, and more powerful than most of the game's bosses, only rivaled in strength by the final boss.

"'. . . [O]r that annoying *EHHH* noise when someone got poisoned.' [Wait, I've heard that noise before . . .]" refers to the very irritating in-game sound when a character is poisoned. The sound was possibly identical to a 1980s alarm clock going off. Ario had heard it before when his alarm clock went off, waking him to the start of his adventure.

"'Well . . . yeah, but, I mean, you got pretty popular after that magazine giveaway though,'" refers to the giveaway featured in the *Nintendo Power* magazine, which included the *Dragon Warrior* game. Nintendo® distributed the game for free to subscribers of *Nintendo Power*. With a year's subscription priced at $20, subscribers could get the $50 game at a deep discount. The promotion resulted in *Nintendo Power* gaining 500,000 new subscribers.[20]

"'If I've told you once, I've told you a thousand times, I was on a quest in a foreign land. That was going great; I came over here—had to change the name to avoid infringing on a trademark, so I lost a little goodwill that way —but I'm sure there'll be a sequel if you know what I mean.

[20] Wikipedia contributors. (2024, February 12). Dragon Quest (video game). In Wikipedia. Retrieved February 12, 2024, from https://en.wikipedia.org/wiki/Dragon_Quest_(video_game)

Nothing final about what I'm doing and, who knows, maybe I'll give that quest a go again.'" There is a lot to unpack here (and credit goes to the *U Can Beat Video Games* YouTube channel for this backstory). The *Dragon Warrior* title was adopted for the English language release of the game known as *Dragon Quest* in Japan. Enix made this name change to avoid trademark infringement with a pen-and-paper RPG game of the same name. Following the success of *Dragon Quest* on the Famicom in Japan, Square decided to develop an RPG for the NES. The development team created *Final Fantasy* and settled on the word "final," partly because if the game failed it would likely be Square's last developed game.[21]

"'Final, huh? Yeah, I don't think so. Trust me, in time, I'm gonna be far too big for this land,'" refers to two things: the numerous spin-offs and sequels in the *Final Fantasy* series, and more importantly, how Sony's PlayStation CD-ROM, with its far larger storage capacity and vastly higher-quality audio compared to Nintendo's® antiquated cartridge system on the Nintendo 64 allowed for significant advancements. The release of the immensely popular *Final Fantasy VII* in 1997 on PlayStation, marked the (albeit temporary) end to *Final Fantasy*'s decade long-run on Nintendo's® consoles.

"'Did I ever tell you about that little cemetery in that little town of Elfheim? The tombstone reads: HERE LIES ERDRICK. You would think such a great man would have a bit better burial place, no?' 'Nope, I know that tombstone, it reads: HERE LIES LINK. No idea who that is, but that's not the great hero from the past himself. Maybe this Link character is a hero elsewhere, but not in Alefgard,'" refers to the Alefgard tombstone in the original Japanese version of *Final Fantasy* on the Famicom. The tombstone reads, "Here lies

[21] "Dragon Warrior NES - ULTIMATE GUIDE". U Can Beat Video Games. URL: https://www.youtube.com/watch?v=IZ5bSqRWrCY Accessed Date: February 8, 2024

Link," but for the US version on the NES, "Link" was changed to "Erdrick"—a reference to the *Dragon Quest* series. But the subsequent remakes of *Final Fantasy* reference Link. Link is referred to as a "hero" in his story arch.

"'Thy night is getting long in thy tooth, dost thou wisheth to retire to our respective inns? . . . Or maybe you could pitch a tent?'" refers to both games utilizing the inn to recover hit points (HP) and magic points (MP) for their characters. In *Dragon Warrior*, players can only save their game by speaking to the king (with an example of how the king might sound), while in *Final Fantasy*, players have multiple means to save their progress, such as a tent, a cabin, or a house while outdoors. And 'pitch a tent' has its own meaning, of course.

"'Well, at least my tent allows me to save my progress. Oh, excuse me, I mean," an air of pretentiousness lay thick in his voice now. "Will thou tell me now of the deeds, so they won't be forgotten? Thy deeds have been recorded on the Imperial Scrolls of Honor,'" refers to the verbatim words spoken by the king when he offers to save the Hero's game progress in *Dragon Warrior.*

"'Is that the one where you switched alignment with a party member so that he got rubbed instead of you?'" refers to the battle with Astos, where his first casted spell is RUB, an instant KO spell. Due to the mechanics of party order, Astos will likely cast RUB at the team member in the top position (which is usually where the fighter is located). By switching party order, the player can "sacrifice" the most expendable party member to the effects of the RUB spell.

"'Right, right, and then that was used to get something to wake the sleeping prince. I think we all know how the wake a sleeping prince story goes,'" refers to returning the crystal to the blind witch, Matoya, which is rewarded after defeating Astos. In exchange for the crystal, Matoya trades the most powerful herb (enabling her to regain her sight, too). The magical herb has the effect of counteracting the sleeping curse Astos placed on the prince. Additionally, it is a reference to the standard fairy tale that a kiss from a prince can wake a sleeping princess (if you don't know the story, check out *Saved by the Bell* season four episode twenty, "Snow White and the Seven Dorks").

"'Gaia, huh? Good luck with that. That place is alllll an illusion,'" refers to the SNES game *Illusion of Gaia*.

"'. . . [A]s for me-eth surely dost thou wonder. I'm off to Rimuldar . . . to get some puff-puff!'" refers to a woman in the town of Rimuldar who sells "puff-puff" in the Japanese Famicom version of *Dragon Quest*. In the Japanese version, puff-puff is offered by beautiful woman of ill-repute and is also an action that female adventures can use to beguile enemy monsters into inaction, often involving posing with their chest thrust forward.[22] However, in the North American NES version, the same woman sells tomatoes instead. What a letdown.

"I'm distracted when a young ladd, blanketed in lime green, flashes before me," refers to the character and his outfit in *Bionic Commando*. In the game's instruction manual, the character is only known as "Player," but in the game's ending, his name is revealed to be "Ladd."

"Grappling with what I'm seeing, I come to understand he has a mechanical arm," refers to Ladd's mechanical arm, which is equipped with grappling gun. This is one of the few games where the player cannot jump; instead, the grappling hook must always be used to cross gaps and climb ledges.

". . . ([T]hat's pretty rad, I think) . . ." refers to the Game Boy version retelling of *Bionic Commando*, where the character is named "Rad."

---

[22] Laudati, L. (n.d.). Dragon Quest's Puff-Puff Joke Explained. TheGamer. Retrieved February 9, 2024, from https://www.thegamer.com/dragon-quest-puff-puff-joke-explained/#:~:text=One%20of%20the%20recurring%20aspects,with%20their%20chest%20thrust%20forward

". . . [W]hich allows him to swing by (on his command, originally) any albatros encumbering his progress," refers to the title *Bionic Commando*. In the game Ladd is trying to stop the Albatros (the word, albatross, is spelled with a second 's') project.

"'. . . A master plan, diabolical in its intentions, a plan so badd. Me, like a ton of bricks it hit, learned, have I to resurrect a man so vile, it must be killt. You've got to get out of this base, for it will explod in sixty seconds.'" There is a lot to unpack here. Like many early NES games, *Bionic Commando* originated from Japanese versions with notable differences. In the Japanese version, the antagonists are the Nazis, but they were referred to as the "Badds" in the US version. Additionally, the leader of the villains was originally named Weizmann but was changed to Killt. The Nazis' plan in the Japanese version is to resurrect Adolf Hitler, his in-game likeness remained in the US version, but his name was changed to Master D. According to the *U Can Beat Video Games* YouTube channel, the original Famicom release of *Bionic Commando* was titled (loosely translated) *Hitler's Resurrection Top Secret*.[23] After the player destroys Hitler's helicopter (with accompanying imagery of Hitler's exploding face), the next area features this text: "This base will 'explod' in 60 seconds. Evacuate right away."

". . . [P]assing some burning oil barrels (what an odd choice to heat the place) and a broken ladder . . ." refers to the burning oil barrels that populate some stages of *Donkey Kong*.

"Before me, a bunch of guys dressed in black suits with matching fedoras. They were not interested in me, though, as they popped in and out of rooms and hopped on and off doorless elevators (don't let OSHA know about those). There's a lot of action here; it's a busy place," refers

---

[23] "Bionic Commando NES - ULTIMATE GUIDE". U Can Beat Video Games. URL https://www.youtube.com/watch?v=YjsYYSYI4lw Accessed Date: February 18, 2024

to *Elevator Action*.

"Maybe they're looking for someone else? I hear a loud bang—was that a gunshot?—then glass breaking as something comes crashing down. The lights go out momentarily but are back on a few seconds later. In a collection of purple doors, a single red one stands out to me," refers to elements of *Elevator Action*.

". . . [A] group of goons ease too close to me . . ." refers to *The Goonies II*.

". . . [W]ho move at a snail's pace—or is it a sloth's pace?" refers to the character named "Sloth" in *The Goonies* movie.

"Then they start excessively knocking on every wall, floor, and ceiling imaginable," refers to elements of *The Goonies II*, where many of the game's secrets and items are uncovered by knocking on or hammering the walls, floors, and ceilings.

". . . ([W]hile the fat one pulls out a candy bar)—maybe rooting for . . ." refers to the Baby Ruth candy bar Chunk shares with Sloth in the movie.

". . . [H]e closes one-eye—will he do what I think he's going to do . . ." refers to the goonies discovering a treasure map, which takes them on an exhilarating adventure to find the long-lost fortune of the legendary 17th-century pirate, "One-Eyed Willy."

". . . [G]o into the fray—tell each one to be careful . . ." refers to the movie's antagonists, the Fratelli crime family.

"That never-say-die attitude . . ." refers to the movie character Mikey's saying, "Goonies never say die."

"I'll give them their time down there," refers to another Mikey quote from the movie, "It's our time down here."

"'Heyyy . . . youuu . . . guyyyyyys!'" refers to Sloth's iconic saying. Sloth belts out the classic line while hoisting the tied-up Fratelli brothers off the deck of the pirate ship.

". . . [I]t's a matte black room with a less-than-lustrous gold finish . . ." refers to the iconic Tengen line of games; games like *Tetris* and the *R.B.I. Baseball* franchise. Their cartridges flaunted a distinct appearance, almost as a tongue-out to the square, blocky gray cartridges of Nintendo®. Tengen's cartridge design, with its rounded matte-black shell featuring a gold label, paid homage to the original Atari cartridges.

". . . ([D]istinct from the shiny gold finishes I've seen elsewhere)," refers to the beautiful gleaming gold cartridges of *The Legend of* Zelda and *Zelda II: The Adventure of Link*.

"I see a mix of ghosts, demons, grunts, and more. Walls and barriers—some displaying cracks—in every direction create a labyrinth-like office space . . ." refers to elements of *Gauntlet*.

". . . [I]nadvertently crushing a pile of skulls and bones. The ghosts start to disappear, one by one," refers to the enemy generators in *Gauntlet*. A heap of skulls and bones will spawn ghosts. The number of skulls—whether one, two, or three—determines both the quantity and resilience of the enemies generated. It's crucial to eliminate these generators to stop the continuous spawning of more enemies.

". . . [U]ntil finally, a figure—a human figure—emerges. His vibrant green attire immediately catches my eye, and his archer's cap boasts a single prominent red plume jutting out of its fold," refers to the Elf character in *Gauntlet*.

"I can tell he was a bit dandy-looking before," refers to *Gauntlet*, which is based on the Atari 800 game, *Dandy*.

". . . [B]ut all his speeding about . . ." refers to the Elf character's top-tier speed in the game. His speed is a very strong asset because he can outrun most enemies (and teammates), ensuring he reaches food, treasure chests, and other items ahead of fellow players in cooperative play.

". . . [A] bit gaunt. "Let me . . ." refers to *Gauntlet*.

"'. . . For the stage, it you must conquest or perish,'" refers to the Elf character's name, Questor.

"'. . . Time's running out.'" "Ahh, I get it, just like those treasure rooms," refers to the urgency of exiting a treasure room before the timer expires to replenish a player's health meter and to receive a password.

"'. . . [H]ope it's not the one that takes you back to the start,'" refers to the top-right exit in Level 80 of *Gauntlet*. Using the exit will send you back to the title screen. The player is warned about it in the *Gauntlet* instruction manual: "At the higher levels of the game, explores report that there are fake exits—it looks like an exit but doesn't work! Apparently, there is a real exit somewhere though."'"Don't worry, you'll get there . . . eventually," refers to *Gauntlet's* difficulty level. The arcade version of the game lacked a definitive ending, and arcade games simply made more money when more quarters were dropped into them. How do you maximize revenue without raising the price to play from one quarter to two? Build a game with no ending, thus encouraging players to keep going. Once the players had played all existing levels, the game cleverly recycled old levels by flipping them horizontally and vertically.

"'I assume you can shoot diagonally, right? Not like that pussy, Thor!'" refers to the limitations of the Warrior character, Thor, who despite his strength and good armor, cannot throw his axe diagonally through narrow sections of walls like how other characters can attack. This nuance significantly hampers the Warrior's effectiveness in long-distance combat compared to the other three characters.

"*Errr-ruhhhhh*," refers to the very distinct nourishment sound when a player eats food.

". . . [F]ollowed shortly after by a jarring buzzing one," refers to the stun floors. They are electrified floor tiles that emit a harsh buzzing noise when touched, temporarily paralyzing the player and rendering them unable to move or shoot for a few seconds. An effective hack to eliminate the paralyzing effect is to pause the game; upon resuming, the paralysis is gone.

"... I see a green door with 'CIC' in white raised lettering displayed against a black nameplate. . . . [B]ut it's locked," refers to Nintendo's® "lockout chip." Formally called the Checking Integrated Circuit, the chip is part of a system known as 10NES, whereby the chip uses a key to check if the game is authentic and if the game is in the same region as the console. The lockout chip prevented unlicensed companies' software from playing on an NES. This was done in part to control the third-party software development that diluted the home console market due to a lack of publishing control. A lack of publishing control was one reason for the video game crash of 1983. Green, white, and black refer to the colors of the actual chip.[24]

". . . [W]hich contain written general instructions for bypassing the lock. Outmaneuvering . . ." refers to the American video game publisher and developer Tengen. Several developers released their games without Nintendo's approval by using workarounds. Tengen (a subsidiary of Atari Games) had the most well-known workaround because they copied the CIC chip, thus bypassing the lockout.

"With the directions, it if I, you, US can copy right off I cease to be stopped by this door . . ." refers to how Tengen figured out how to bypass the 10NES chip. They illegally obtained documents from the US Copyright Office under the guise of claiming that it was required to defend against present infringement claims in a legal case. Tengen used the information obtained to duplicate the function of the 10NES chip.

". . . I'm now standing on a large white mat labeled "EXIT" in big red letters; I'm certain it wasn't there when I approached the door," refers to the exit tiles in *Gauntlet*.

[24] Wikipedia contributors. (2024, March 7). CIC (Nintendo). In Wikipedia. Retrieved March 7, 2024, from https://en.wikipedia.org/wiki/CIC_(Nintendo).

Exit tiles are the only way to progress to the next level, but some levels require specific events to uncover an exit tile. For example, the player might need to shoot away a wall to reveal an exit.

"I see a door handle, so I grabb it," refers to the Rabbit chip designed by Tengen. Its design duplicated the function of the 10NES chip, thus bypassing Nintendo's® lockout allowing for Tengen's unlicensed games to play on the NES. *Gauntlet* was one of three Tengen games released in licensed and unlicensed versions (the other two are *R.B.I. Baseball* and *Pac-Man*).

". . . [T]o reveal '101' inscribed in place of 'CIC' on the nameplate," refers to the completion of *Gauntlet's* one hundred levels. In this story, the 101st level symbolizes the completion of *Gauntlet,* bringing Ario into the next part of the building, closer to his interview.

"Since I'm not back at the entrance, I suppose this must be the right place," refers to the *Gauntlet* fake exit Easter egg referenced earlier.

". . . [L]ots of gray, a dull gray—filled with brick and steel, all the same monotonous hue. Nevertheless, to spruce it up, I guess there is some vegetation and signs of life scattered around. . . . I navigate through a maze of corridors. . . . At one point, I pass a large aquarium teeming with jumping fish and little, tiny squids," refers to the environment of World 8 - 4 in *Super Mario Bros*.

". . . [S]ome pretty fiery looking plants in the corner. They don't have teeth, do they? Into that plant, I won't peer aroun' an' have a look," refers to the fireball spitting Piranha Plants in *Super Mario Bros*.

"She's a real battle-axe of a woman," refers to Bowser, who has the axe behind him, which Mario uses to sever the bridge cable.

"Jump, man, I tell myself—she's breathing fire," refers to the original iteration of the Mario character, which was in *Donkey Kong*. He was called Jump Man. Bowser breathes fire so the player must jump over it to avoid being hit.

"... [S]he wants to drop the hammer on me really quick," refers to Bowser throwing hammers at Mario.

"Quick hands—I didn't even see her make a throwing motion," refers to the hammers released by Bowser without even a throwing motion of his hands.

"Fortunately, they go right over my head. I push closer. (Note to self: when issuing HR forms, toss them directly *at* your future employee, not on a looping trajectory)," refers to the trajectory of Bowser's hammer throws, which gives Mario an easy path to run under them.

"I approach her with caution, knowing that if I get hit, it will knock me down a size, but I won't be dead," refers to Mario, in his larger state, taking a hit that will reduce his size but not kill him.

"She jumps out of her chair—I didn't think someone that size could jump that high—but it gives me an opening .... Just like that, I slip right past her," refers to defeating Bowser by running under him when he jumps (Bowser can also be defeated with fireballs).

"The snarling beast drops out of sight," refers to Bowser plummeting into the lava after Mario cuts the bridge cable.

"... [A] world anew," refers to the last line spoken by Peach. It is displayed on the end screen: "Your quest is over. We present you a new quest. Push Button B to Select A World."

"... [B]ut I'll live. Oy, you'll stop staring at me at some point, right ..." refers to Princess Peach's design, which *Popeye's* Olive Oyl loosely inspired.[25]

"She exudes an air of royalty ... not that of a queen, but more akin to her young, elegant daughter," refers to a

---

[25] The Fact Site. (n.d.). Princess Peach Facts. Retrieved February 9, 2024, from https://www.thefactsite.com/princess-peach-facts/

princess, as in Princess Peach.

". . . [H]aving no clue what that gal who belongs not working a desk job is saying to me about genies," refers to Galoob's Game Genie, a revolutionary cheat device in the world of video games (which extended beyond the NES). Originating with the NES, it was essentially a cartridge adapter, allowing players to integrate an NES game cartridge with the Game Genie before slotting the ensemble into the NES console. The device allowed players to input cheat codes to modify various aspects of games. I remember using Game Genie for SNES to beat *Final Fight*. "Jeans are acceptable in this workplace, but genies are not," refers to FAM in this story not permitting a device to make gameplay easier.

"My palms are sweaty (but for different reasons)," refers to Ario's palms being sweaty due to being in the presence of a pretty woman, not the player's.

"She reminds me of a girl, Pauline, whom I once had a crush on, but not anymore," refers to the character Pauline in the 1981 arcade game version of *Donkey Kong*, whom Mario (known as Jump Man) must rescue. The damsel-in-distress idea of Pauline in *Super Mario Bros.* was replaced by the character who came to be known as Princess Peach.

". . . [H]ow I always hated my father, Otto, for giving me his first name as my middle," refers to the construction of Ario's name as Miyam Otto, which refers to the "father of Nintendo®," Shigeru Miyamoto.

"She gestured toward a gray box, roughly the size of a VCR, which also bore a striking resemblance to one. It featured a flip-up top, much like a VCR, where you could place your suggestion inside," refers to the designers of the NES aiming to make their product look and function similarly to a VHS player. The approach intended to make the product familiar to the American market. The NES looks quite different from its predecessor, the Famicom.

"'Us lower employees have a little mantra here, which we shortened to 'fax-and-a-do,''" refers to *Faxanadu* (pronounced fa-zan-a-do). The name is a portmanteau of Famicom and Xanadu. Xanadu came from the Japanese game *Dragon Slayer II: Xanadu*, which went unreleased in the North American market.[26] The game utilizes a password system known as "mantras."

"'But once I didn't have to do it myself, I sent in a fax, and the drinking fountain got fixed,'" refers to the plot of *Faxanadu*. The hero returns to find his town in disrepair and nearly abandoned. The Elven King explains that the town's water fountain, their life source, has run dry, and the remaining water has been poisoned, thus setting the player off on his/her quest.

"'M dot Ario,'" means the nametag for Miyam Ario would be M.ARIO (obviously).

"'I guess I should tell you that everyone outside of the office calls me something else, but in here, I keep that 'totes to -uh- like myself.' Oddly, she spoke with a heavy valley girl accent at the end . . ." refers to the period before 1994 when the character was exclusively recognized as Princess Peach within Japan. Beyond Japan, she was simply referred to as "Princess Toadstool." However, the name "Peach" began to gain traction in everyday *Mario* dialogue, becoming more prevalent in 1996 with the release of Nintendo® 64's *Super Mario 64*.[Refer to footnote 25 for citation.]

"But you've come this far, so it's not like we're going to send you elsewhere," refers to Mario defeating Bowser in other castle worlds (the # - 4 worlds), but then being told, "Our princess is in another castle."

"My journey to this pivotal point was met with challenges, but an impossible TASk, it was not. If I have to make this commute again, I think I can do it more quickly," refers to the concept of speedrunning a game and using the tool-assisted speedrun (TAS) techniques.

---

[26] "Faxanadu NES - ULTIMATE GUIDE". U Can Beat Video Games. URL: https://www.youtube.com/watch?v=8vEyiAs-fbY Accessed Date: March 16, 2024

"Mr. Gunpei," and "Mr. Shigeru," refer to video game designer Gunpei Yokoi, who is considered the father of handheld gaming, and to video game designer, producer, and game director Shigeru Miyamoto, who is regarded as one of the most accomplished and influential designers in video game history.

GAME OVER

Author's Note on *Final Fantasy / Dragon Warrior*

I wanted to include this piece after the *Final Fantasy / Dragon Warrior* section, but I went off on a personal video game memory tangent, so I had to relocate it here.

In the NES days, I didn't like RPGs (at least, at first). I have never played any game in the *Final Fantasy* series on the NES or any other system. I remember the immense popularity of *FFVII* on PlayStation, but I was an N64 kid. I watched some friends play *FFVII* (at Ian Johnson's house), but stepping into the middle of an RPG game probably defines being lost. Side note: I loved *Metal Gear* and can still remember the first time I saw the commercial for *Metal Gear Solid*. I was so excited . . . and then I saw it was for Play-Station. I was so upset. In my research of *Final Fantasy,* I realized my regret for not playing it back in the NES days. I enjoyed the walkthrough video and could tell it was a game I would have enjoyed.

I was one of those 500,000 *Nintendo Power* magazine subscribers who got *Dragon Warrior* for free. I played it for about five minutes and hated it. Looking back, I was too young to appreciate the turn-based strategy style of gaming that RPGs are known for. In my earlier video-game-playing days, I needed more instant action and gratification that came with games like *Zelda*, *Mario*, and *Metroid*. It was near the end of the NES run (and maybe the SNES had been out already), but I was bored and looking for something to do, so I gave *Dragon Warrior* a second shot. I fell in love with it. I played it non-stop, traversing across Alefgard, leveling up, and accumulating a ton of gold (not via the gold hack, either). The crazy thing is, I never beat the game . . . because I never went to face the Dragonlord. I had the handout that showed what XP points you had to obtain to level up. I can't remember, but I think the handout went up to level ninety-nine, so I thought I had to be that high to fight the Dragonlord—not that I wouldn't be allowed to, but rather, I wouldn't be strong enough. Then, one day, I just stopped playing it.

That thought still gets me to this day. Every single video game you've ever played, there was a last time you ever played it (and most of the time, you never knew it). The most recent game I played for real was *LoZ: Breath of the Wild*. I didn't do everything in it; I certainly wasn't going to find 900 korok seeds, but I did beat Ganon. Being aware of video game playing finality now, I did reflect on what would be my last time playing *BotW*. I hopped on my horse (fittingly named Epona . . . but she was one of a few in the stable) high in the snowy mountains of Hebra and trotted down the trials to and through Hyrule's different regions, just taking it all in before beating Ganon relatively easily.

To come full circle from most often not knowing the last time I played so many video games, I do remember the first time I played many games. Not so much with the NES, though I do remember eagerly awaiting the release of *Zelda II: The Adventure of Link* . . . only to hate the game. I was expecting a duplication of my favorite NES game but with new items to find and new dungeons to explore. I was very disappointed, but years later, as an adult, I played it on an emulator, and I liked it and appreciated its stylistic departure from the original.

I can see myself sitting on the living room floor of a couple of childhood friends' homes: at Peter Blaise's house watching him play *Mega Man 2* (and him telling me there's a *Mega Man* "one," but it's really hard) and *Gremlins (*actually titled *Gremlins 2: The New Batch)*. Maybe that was a movie tie-in to make the video game version a "2." Sitting in Marty Majda's basement watching him play *The Goonies II*, I wondered why I had never heard of *The Goonies* (or a similar title indicating it was the first video game in the series), but that was because the first one was a little-known game for Nintendo's® PlayChoice-10 arcade machine. Marty could get every item in the game and rescue every Goonie, but he could never find the candle (I just looked it up, and you must punch an old lady five times to get the candle—go figure). My neighbor, Gentry Crosby, came over to my house, where I watched him beat Mike Tyson.

I can see myself opening the SNES for Christmas (and I remember getting the NES for Christmas, too, but that was more a gift for my brother. I remember looking at the box and the stack of games and not knowing what it was); the first time playing *Super Mario World*, *Pilotwings*, or *Sim City* (my first three games on that system); the first time I dropped *The Legend of Zelda: A Link to the Past* into the SNES (one of my all-time favorites and probably number one for me on the SNES). While at Lincoln Mall (demolished in 2017), I can see myself pleading with my parents to buy me *Super Castlevania IV*. After a bit of debating (I remember part of their reasoning was that they had bought my brother something, so they felt more inclined to buy me something), they made an extremely wise decision. The graphics in the rotating room level blew me away. Speaking of graphics, the first time I saw the falling snow in the Gorilla Glacier levels of *Donkey Kong Country* was amazing. I hated the "Mine Cart Carnage" level in DKC but then grew to love it. I can recall being truly STUCK in a video game with no idea what to do (and that game was one of my all-time favorites, *Super Metroid*) until I randomly decided to lay a power bomb in the glass tube. *Secret of Mana* was another RPG game I grinded* at, only to stop playing it, never to beat it, but I did get to watch my junior high friend, Dan Cesaro, beat it, so that counts for something. I can picture looking at the *Secret of Mana* box art with excitement and anticipation for my next fantasy adventure. The essence of fantasy adventure video game box art is how a still picture can capture the imagination, serve as a gateway to an immersive world, and promise an epic journey ahead (but we all know sometimes that promise didn't deliver). Holding *Secret of Mana* in my hands (I bought it at Best Buy), I saw this group of small characters in the foreground overshadowed by a majestic and awe-inspiring tree, staring with wonder at it, as they (and I) were to be drawn into a world of mystique and wonder. Side note: I remember Dan having *U.N. Squadron* (a super fun game) and how there was a boss battle I could never get past.

There were plenty of sports games, too, and the best ones were played with friends (or my dad). My dad never played video games. Unlike parents who can play with their kids today, my dad didn't grow up in the time of video games, and he was older and married with kids during the popularity of the 1970's arcade, so he missed that wave, too; it wasn't anything to which he was accustom, but *R.B.I. Baseball* on the NES was simple enough for us to have "a pitch and a catch." For sports, it was mostly *Madden* with some hockey sprinkled in. I remember my junior high friend, Matt Betourney, and I would play co-op as the Steelers (it was the mid-nineties, and their defense was legit). I would handle the D-lineman, and he'd control the secondary. Mostly, he'd play as Rod Woodson and come unblocked off the corner. I'd move D-lineman around, and one time, I placed a defensive end in the A-gap. I timed the snap perfectly and shot through, blasting Dave Kreig for the immediate sack. He lets out a yell (the ambulance didn't come out knocking over bystanders—that was in the 1992

*my editor suggested "grounded," but that doesn't feel right to me.

version). We checked the injury report, and Dave Kreig had a dislocated shoulder. It was an exciting time for two junior high boys.

My other fond *Madden* memory is when my dad's childhood friend, Ken Venuso, who moved to Texas as an adult, would come to visit with his family. Like most times, when kids are around other kids, they don't know that well, it takes a bit of time to warm up to each other, but two games got us there: *Madden* and *Mario Kart*. Chris and I were closer in age, and Nick was younger (RIP Nick), and like my older brother and his friend, Dave, before me, the younger ones would watch while the older kids played. Chris and I had some epic *Mario Kart* battles. I remember one time in Battle Course 4, Chris and I triggered every single question mark before either of us had lost, so the entire question mark board was repopulated. First time for everything. Speaking of battles, but first . . .

Major League Baseball Featuring Ken Griffey Jr. on N64 was a classic and my favorite baseball game. I played an entire 162-game season with the White Sox, and I'm pretty sure I hit eighty-four home runs with Frank Thomas. I was also trying for a 200 RBI season with him, but I came up short, maybe around 180 - 190 RBIs. I also would trade for every knuckleballer in the game (Tim Wakefield was my ace). As for N64, I can recall getting the system (which no longer came with a *Mario* game, unlike its two predecessors), and having the system for a week or two without a game to play on it. Finally, Target got a shipment of *Super Mario 64*. They had about eighty copies of the game behind a locked case. Knowing what I know now, I should have bought an extra copy, left it unopened, and sealed it safely away in a box.

Goldeneye 007 multiplayer. Enough said, and no using Odd Job!

I remember the first real, in-depth video game conversation I had, and it came at a time when I was no longer an NES-playing kid. It was in high school, and Matt Heabel and I were sitting in my car in the parking lot of the Park Forest Library. We had dropped off Joe Drevlow for something he needed to do in the library. [Side note: I recall going to the library to use their internet to look up *Goldeneye 007* tips and tricks.] If there was no need for us to go into a library, then why bother? So, we stayed in the car and chatted. It was a revelation to me that—a decade-plus after their releases—someone else loved the same games that I did. I mean, I knew video games were extremely popular, but to actually discuss our respective love for childhood games (like me, *Zelda* and *Metroid* were two of Matt's favorites) was a conversation I hadn't had before. And to bring it full circle, Matt was a *Dragon Warrior* fan. I told him the story of why I never (even attempted to) beat the game. The next time I was at his house, I watched him beat the Dragonlord. In the days before YouTube, that was your only chance to see what to do or how something was done; somebody had to show you. We both shared with much anticipation the release of *The Legend of Zelda: Ocarina of Time*. I can see the opening intro of Link on his horse at dawn, galloping across the plains of Hyrule while the peaceful music playing in the background slowly builds. I was in college, and I stayed for the four-week summer course so that I could knock out a non-elective geography 101 class. The uniquely dark *Majora's Mask* occupied a lot of my free time. I remember calling the Nintendo® helpline with questions about *Majora's Mask*; I think my monthly phone bill, typically in the low teens, was $35 because of those calls.

I could go on with more video game memories, but those are the most impactful to me (and it just popped into my head using Game Genie to beat *Final Fight*). On the great *Fly on the Wall with Dana Carvey and David Spade* podcast, Dana Carvey relayed how producer Lorne Michaels said that a person's favorite Saturday Night Live cast is when s/he was around twelve or thirteen years old. That theory aligns withmy favorite cast, the bad boys of SNL: Farley, Sandler, Rock, Spade, and Schneider who occupied the 8H studio in the early to mid-nineties. To me, an SNL favorite cast theory is a time and place occurrence, just like with video games. If asked, "What's your favorite video game?" is your answer strictly gameplay-based, or is your answer because of the vivid memories your favorite game created, the relationships formed from co-op or pass-and-play gameplay, or maybe the friends with which you experienced those cherished memories?

My favorite video game memories are from a time and place of different stages of my youth: as a young kid just trying to navigate the hand-eye coordination of the controller while responding to what I was seeing on the TV screen before me; as an adolescent appreciating the beauty and the stories unfolding in pixelated art that brought friends together (and prompted a few arguments, fights, and curse outs, too); and as a young adult growing up [debatable] in college and on to other less childish / more adult things (but really, playing video games isn't a kids-only pastime), yet video games were commonplace, and multiplayer games were a great way to start the evening.

My most impactful video game memory happened not too long ago, and it's one not from my childhood but from my son's. I was five when *Super Mario Bros.* found its way into our household. The same game was available on the *Wii Virtual Console*, and I sat there watching my five-year-old son, Josh, play *Super Mario Bros.* I was thirty-five then, and I watched my son play the same game I played thirty years prior at the same age I was. It was a beautiful, surreal moment that showed how the same video game could forge enduring connections across familial generations, transcending age barriers and shaping shared experiences.

Attention “Gunters,”*
Did you think I would explain *every* Easter egg? Let’s just say the most well-hidden eggs are still unfound. And in true video game fashion, you need to find them to unlock the next level. Check out retro84book.com/easteregg for more info. Happy hunting!

*and “Gunters” refers to . . .?

Epilogue

I'm not a writer. What I did with this story is something I'm very proud of. The entire content of the story was my own. I've written tens of thousands of emails (so that should count for something, right?), some more formal than others, but I've never put pen to paper (rather, fingers to keyboard) to craft a story. It was tough, but I did have fun doing it, bringing back some wonderful memories of my youth—of far simpler times. I wish I could have made this story longer. I watched some game walkthroughs where I came away thinking, "I got nothing. I can't tell a story here." A lot of the game references in the final stage were simply because of that—it's hard to devote an entire level to *Duck Hunt*.

I wish I could have made a "real" book, if that makes sense—too many words for a short story but not enough for a novel. Including the "Easter Eggs Explained" section would push it into the novel category, but that feels cheap. I believe this book falls into the novella category. I wanted it to be longer, but I'm happy with the finished product, and if it's a good, tight, concise story, then so be it. That's the length it's going to be. I also think that a short book might be the route to go in today's very short attention span society. I'm sure I missed some perfect Easter egg or reference or pun (and probably multiple times over) that I'll regret having missed or will leave me saying, "Why didn't I think of that?" or "I can't believe I missed that one."

I like to read, but I'm not fond of long books. I think most long books (those over 200-ish pages or so) contain a lot of fluff and filler. Maybe I'm just not a good reader, and what I think is filler is actually good material that I missed the point on. Even as a kid in school, my reading comprehension was probably my weakest area. My mind would always drift when reading; it still happens today, but I'm more aware of it now. I'm aware to the point where I'll go back and reread what I wasn't paying attention to. With that said (written), I could have had somebody punch up this writing, or I could have looked for areas to pump in some fluff (but then I'd be a fluffer, and I don't want that job), but that would feel cheap, and I think it would devalue the story. I wanted to deliver a nice, tight story regardless of the page count, and I tried to cram a shit-ton of Easter eggs in it, to boot. I hope I delivered. To that point, I will turn the rest of this epilogue over to a far more skilled writer.

As the dust settled from the wreckage of the Video Game Crash of 1983, the once-thriving video game industry lay in ruins. Consumer trust had been shattered, countless companies had gone bankrupt, and retailers had been left with vast inventories of unsellable games. It was a grim time for those who had witnessed the meteoric rise of video gaming, only to see it fall so spectacularly. However, from the ashes of this digital apocalypse, a phoenix was about to emerge, ready to breathe new life into the lifeless industry. This savior came in the form of a Japanese company known as Nintendo.

Nintendo had been watching the industry's downfall from afar, and they were determined not to make the same mistakes. With a vision for quality, innovation, and a unique approach to gaming, they introduced the Nintendo Entertainment System (NES) in North America in 1985. This was a home console that didn't just play games; it was a gaming experience carefully curated to ensure excellence in both gameplay and presentation.

At the heart of the NES's success was "Super Mario Bros.," a revolutionary platformer that redefined video games and set a new standard for excellence. Players were captivated by the charming Italian plumber, Mario, and his quest to rescue Princess Peach from the clutches of the villainous Bowser. The game's impeccable design, engaging gameplay, and memorable characters rekindled the love for video games among players young and old.

Nintendo's approach to game development was transformative. They implemented a strict quality control process, ensuring that only the finest titles made it to their platform. Third-party developers were required to meet Nintendo's high standards, preventing a flood of inferior games from diluting the market.

In addition to this, Nintendo introduced a novel concept that would become a hallmark of their success – the "Nintendo Seal of Quality." This seal assured players that the game they were purchasing had met rigorous standards and was worth their investment. It was a symbol of trust and reliability in an industry still scarred by the crash.

The resurrection of the video game industry had begun, and Nintendo's NES became a household staple, selling millions of units and revitalizing consumer interest in video gaming. Soon, other companies like Sega would follow suit, leading to a new era of competition and innovation in the gaming world.

The Video Game Crash of 1983 was a dark chapter in the industry's history, but it was also a necessary reckoning. It forced the industry to confront its own excesses and shortcomings, ultimately paving the way for a brighter future. Nintendo's role in this revival cannot be overstated, as they not only resurrected a lifeless industry but also set a new standard for excellence and creativity that continues to influence gaming to this day. From those uncertain times emerged a gaming landscape richer, more diverse, and more exciting than ever before, thanks to the resilience and innovation of those who refused to let the game be over.

What you just read was ChatGPT's verbatim response to my question, "Can you write me an epilogue about the video game industry coming out of the video game crash of 1983 and how Nintendo resurrected a lifeless industry?" I asked ChatGPT to give me some information on the video game crash of 1983, and I pulled some content from its answers to bulk up my prologue. ChatGPT generated my front cover image of a boy sitting in front of a 1980's-style TV. I told it, "Give me a drawing of a kid sitting on the floor in the 1980s playing video games on a big wooden box frame TV." It was the first time I've ever used AI; it was somewhat of a mind-opening experience. I went through a few iterations of "big wooden box frame TV" examples of what I wanted, but when I first saw what would become the cover photo, I instantly knew that's what I wanted. I doctored it up a bit, but thanks to ChatGPT for creating it. And thanks to ChatGPT for converting website links into APA citation form, too. Also, Grammarly was a huge help for grammar, punctuation, and sentence structure. Compared to the average American, I think my grammar is pretty good, but Grammarly showed me I have a lot to learn (and now I will copy and paste this sentence into their app . . . 98 overall score with Correctness, Clarity, and Engagement meters full, but the Delivery meter is a bit short).

It's incredible what technology can do. Technology (among some brilliant and driven minds) rescued a nearly dead video game industry, and now it just wrote a far better epilogue to my book than I could have.

<u>Acknowledgements</u>

Thank you to Wikipedia, the various YouTube channels, and fan wiki pages dedicated to these games. In particular, *U Can Beat Video Games* YouTube channel was <u>the most helpful</u> in providing a deep insight into games. While memory served me well for the—or, at least, my—most notable Easter eggs, I needed to pull in multiple areas of research to fully dive into a game and to prove if my memories from thirty-five to forty years ago were correct. Most were, but some were a bit cloudy, and I learned a good amount of something new in the process.

Thank you to Rebecca Demos for her help with the book cover illustration and formatting the book for publication. She is an illustrator for Leap for Literacy, a non-profit organization closing the learning gap in underprivileged schools through reading and writing. Rebecca Demos can be found online under the handle BHillgie, and her books can be found at both Amazon.com and Barnes and Noble. And thanks for her patience with my attention to detail:)

Thank you to Old Quarry Middle School Principal Joe Sweeney (author of *JJ's Toad-Ally Great Adventure*) for his insight on self-publishing, and for connecting me with Rebecca. An additional thank you to Joe for being a great principal who clearly cares about his students.

Thank you to Wayne Pelletier at Resonant Pixel Company LLC for creating the retro84book.com website.

Thank you to my editor, Dan (I don't even know his last name), at WordSharp Editing and Proofreading for editing the "normal" pages. When I gave him my entire book to edit, he declined because "From an editor's point of view, *it's a mess* [emphasis added] . . . this would be nearly impossible for me to edit." At first, his response had me completely worried. I thought my work was trash, but after some thought, I understood why, which made me think, maybe that's a good thing . . . time will tell if it is. Nonetheless, his editing of the "normal" pages was helpful.

A more complete 'Thank you to Grammarly' because it was a huge help in cleaning up grammar, punctuation, and sentence structure. I actually learned a bit~~ in the process o~~f while watching Grammarly do its thing, too. I also learned it doesn't like words like "actually," "finally," "just," "really," and "in fact," to name a few and it made me realize how often I use those types of words in my speech and thoughts. It suggested I remove "in the process of" and replace it with "while," . . . OK, fair enough.

Thank you to my neighbor, Tim Grochocinski, for giving me free legal advice regarding my book cover design replicating an NES box. Because of his generosity, I changed the "Louie G." surname to his.

Thank you to my mom for putting up with my video game-related tantrums, many of which involved excessive cursing and even the occasional (I'm being biased) thrown controller.

Thank you to my brother, Joe, for being the first person to read the (very) rough draft. His enthusiastic "I enjoyed reading it" motivated me to see this project through to completion. I can still see six-year-old me barging into his room to watch him and his friend, Dave Danick, play *Metroid*. If I didn't annoy them, I was allowed to sit quietly and watch . . . until they made fun of my not being able to pronounce my "Rs" at the end of words (i.e., heater, I would pronounce heat-uh), which would drive me from the room crying. And, of course, they would goad me into using such words.*

*after all these years, Joe and Dave are still good friends . . . and they've eased up their teasing of me, too.

About The Author

[Here I go, writing in the third person as if someone else—like a professional 'About the Author' writer—was paid to write a blurb about me.]

While not much of a gamer anymore (because life gets in the way), Mike grew up playing video games. It's probably what he did the most in his youth (and probably a great contributor to him being a fat kid growing up, but we're not here to bash video games and their influence on a sedentary lifestyle), and it generated some of his most excellent childhood and young adulthood memories, too. He now sees his teenage son and the memories he's making with *Fortnite* . . . and Mike is a bit nostalgic for it (and feeling envious of the moments and memories that have slipped into the past). Writing "Retro '84" was an enjoyable and memorable experience for Mike as he grasped for those slowly fading NES memories. Mike still misses reading video game instruction manuals while sitting on the toilet, too.

Mike lives in Lemont, Illinois, with his family. He is a CERTIFIED FINANCIAL PLANNER™ who owns Pensinger Financial, Inc., an honest, straightforward, and transparent financial planning and investment management firm. To learn more about its services, visit pen-fin.com.

www.ingramcontent.com/pod-product-compliance
Lightning Source LLC
LaVergne TN
LVHW010913110826
845149LV00013B/2352

* 9 7 9 8 9 9 0 0 6 7 8 0 6 *